The smile that had begun to spread across his face froze. Something wasn't right. There was something different about her.

Something very different. Her beautiful suntanned face was pale. Her bright blue eyes had shadows. But it was her new curvy body, the one with the unmistakable baby bump, that immediately got his attention. And held it.

"I don't understand…" he began as the wheels in his befuddled brain began to turn. How could this be possible?

Well, he knew how. But why? He'd used protection. They both had.

But that didn't matter right then. What mattered was that Summer looked as if she was about to drop.

"You need to sit down," Alex said as he crossed the grass to where she stood and took her arm to lead her to a seat. "We both need to sit down."

He took the seat closest to hers. He'd known that there was something wrong when Summer had become more adamant about knowing where he was going and when he was returning, but he had never imagined this.

"Why didn't you tell me?" he asked.

Dear Reader,

Sometimes we dream of visiting faraway lands while there are still places to explore in our own backyard, so last summer, I decided to take a road trip around my own state of Florida. We took the old abandoned roads that led to some great forgotten places and we made one unexpected stop for an alligator who had claimed the highway as his own.

The crowning moment of the trip was exploring the island of Key West. With a history full of adventurers, I enjoyed meeting the local people who were welcoming and eager to share their own journey to the island.

It's these same people who make up my Key West medevac helicopter crew. Some were born on the island while others came for work and found a home. Both Alex and Summer originally came to the island for a new start and soon realized that while the island is the home they've always wanted, there is still something missing from their lives. I hope you enjoy their adventure to find that missing piece on their way to their own happily-ever-after.

Best wishes,

Deanne Anders

PREGNANT WITH THE SECRET PRINCE'S BABIES

DEANNE ANDERS

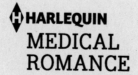

HARLEQUIN
MEDICAL
ROMANCE

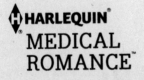

HARLEQUIN®
MEDICAL ROMANCE™

Recycling programs for this product may not exist in your area.

ISBN-13: 978-1-335-73759-5

Pregnant with the Secret Prince's Babies

Copyright © 2022 by Denise Chavers

For questions and comments about the quality of this book, please contact us at CustomerService@Harlequin.com.

Harlequin Enterprises ULC
22 Adelaide St. West, 41st Floor
Toronto, Ontario M5H 4E3, Canada
www.Harlequin.com

Printed in U.S.A.

Deanne Anders was reading romance while her friends were still reading Nancy Drew, and she knew she'd hit the jackpot when she found a shelf of Harlequin Presents in her local library. Years later, she discovered the fun of writing her own. Deanne lives in Florida with her husband and their spoiled Pomeranian. During the day, she works as a nursing supervisor. With her love of everything medical and romance, writing for Harlequin Medical Romance is a dream come true.

Books by Deanne Anders

Harlequin Medical Romance

From Midwife to Mommy
The Surgeon's Baby Bombshell
Stolen Kiss with the Single Mom
Sarah and the Single Dad
The Neurosurgeon's Unexpected Family
December Reunion in Central Park
Florida Fling with the Single Dad

Visit the Author Profile page at Harlequin.com.

This book is dedicated to Jacob, Abigail, Josie, Roman and Molly, who are always eager to share with their teachers that their nana is an author even though they aren't allowed to read her books until they get older.

**Praise for
Deanne Anders**

"This story captivated me. I enjoyed every moment [of] it. This is a great example of a medical romance. Deanne Anders is an amazing writer!"
—*Goodreads* on *The Surgeon's Baby Bombshell*

CHAPTER ONE

"The king is not happy."

Though thousands of miles away, his brother's booming voice ricocheted inside his pounding head like it was a pinball machine.

After spending over twelve hours on a plane, Dr. Alex Leonelli had finally made it home to Key West, leaving behind his life as Alexandro Michael Leonelli, best friend and secret half brother of Crown Prince Nicholas of Soura. The last thing he wanted was to listen to his brother try to lay a guilt trip on him. He'd more than done his duty for his brother. It was only right for Nicholas to get stuck with their father's bad temper after all the trouble he'd been the last five months.

He punched in the code on the front door to Heli-Care's headquarters. He was glad they hadn't changed the code. He was even luckier that he still had a job.

"Sounds like a personal problem," Alex said

as he looked up at the clear sky overhead. The moon and stars were still putting on an early morning show for all the tourists who'd soon be heading home after their night of partying in downtown Key West.

It was so good to be back. He'd missed everything about the small island. Because while the palm trees reminded him of where he had grown up in California and the local beaches reminded him of the Mediterranean ones of his father's small country, Key West was his home. Here he was just Dr. Alex, ER doc and medical chief of Heli-Care's local medevac unit. He liked who he was able to be here.

"You stole out in the middle of the night like you were some common thief," his brother said.

"And whose fault is that? Every time I mentioned heading home you suddenly had a supposed relapse. And don't get me started on all the ways our father tried to keep me there." He didn't have time for this. He only had a few hours before jet lag brought him to a crashing halt. He'd been away for too long and he was ready to get back to work. It was his friend Dylan's hard work covering for him that had helped him keep his job and he knew his crew had been in good hands. But Dylan now had a new wife and needed to get on with his own life. Just like Alex needed to get on with his.

Which was why he'd headed to Heli-Care's base, instead of heading home, or at least that was what he was telling himself. It had absolutely nothing to do with the petite blond registered nurse who, according to the crew schedule, was on an overnight shift right now.

Summer. What was going on with her? With them? And how was he going to fix it?

"It's that girl, isn't it?" his brother said, as if he had just read Alex's mind.

"Just because you bounce between one woman to another doesn't mean that everyone is happy with that life." Alex had never understood his brother's insistence on playing the bad-boy crown prince when he could do so much more with his life.

"You could be if you'd let yourself. And I think she made it pretty clear that she has moved on even if you haven't. How many times does a woman have to refuse your calls for you to get a hint?"

"Shouldn't you be working on your rehab instead of worrying about my love life?" His brother was right, but Alex wasn't ready to admit it. Not yet. Summer had cut all contact between them the moment he had left Key West. When she'd refused his calls and hadn't returned any of his texts, he'd been surprised. Summer wasn't someone who liked a lot of drama in her life. If she was angry, she told you. Her not returning his calls didn't make sense. But he'd had to put aside all of that until his brother's life was out of danger.

"I just hope she's worth making our father angry. You have to know that he's looking for a reason to out you."

"What?" Alex's hand froze on the door handle.

"He wants to acknowledge you as his son, Alex." His brother's voice gave no hint about how he personally felt about his father's plan.

"Isn't it a little late for that? I've played the game of hiding who I am too long to change my life now." And he didn't want to change. Living in Key West as a simple doctor was the life he had dreamed of. No cameras, no reporters, no paparazzi. No one wanting to highlight and criticize everything he did. It was the perfect life for him.

"Besides, we both know the scandal would be bad for all of us," Alex said. If he could only get his brother on his side, maybe they could get his father to see reason.

"Maybe for our father and your mother. But for us? I'd say the benefits will balance out the burden of the media attention," his brother said with his usual nonchalance.

"And what benefit would that be?" His father and brother had never understood his life. Bringing media attention into his life would have direct consequences for his job. How could he work out in the open if he constantly had to be worrying about the paparazzi showing up?

He stepped into the building and entered the multiuse room, where he'd spent many an hour with his crew watching movies and gaming. It was empty—not surprising at this time of the morning. The overnight crew would be catching some downtime before being dispatched to the next call, or the morning crew came in.

The thought of giving up this place, these people, was impossible to consider.

This was where he belonged. Not stashed in some palace with his only patient being a grouchy royal. He rubbed his temples as the aching in his head seemed to magnify with that thought. Leaving the palace when he had had been the right thing for him. He would have lost his mind if he'd stayed another day.

And his timing was perfect. He would have enough time to catch up on some emails before shift change. Then he could see his staff and let them know he was back.

And then there was Summer. He needed her to see that he had returned, just like he'd promised all those months ago. He could only hope that her seeing he had kept his promise to return would help make things right between them.

And if she wanted the details on why he had been gone so long? How would he answer her questions? He'd wanted to tell her about his other life for months before he'd left, but he'd always hesitated, afraid that it would change things between them.

"It's time, Alex," his brother said, startling him. The pounding in his head doubled.

"For what exactly?" He couldn't keep the irritation out of his voice. All of this was his brother's fault. The Crown Prince of Soura should have been taking care of his royal duties instead of chasing his latest daring thrill.

Which was why he had ended up in a critical-care unit with half of his ribs broken, a punctured lung and both his femurs fractured, and as a result, Alex had left Key West without any notice. His lack of explanation meant that Summer had cut all communication between the two of them.

Alex couldn't blame his father for calling him and demanding that he come to his tiny

Mediterranean kingdom of Soura immediately. His brother had needed him.

But so had Summer.

And he didn't understand that. Not really. Summer had always been so independent and so understanding about his job and the crazy hours he worked. He couldn't understand why she had reacted so differently that day. His father's phone call had left no doubt of how urgent it was for him to get to his brother. He'd had no choice. Jeopardizing his job and running out on his crew was not something that he would have ever dreamed of doing. She'd known that. Just like she'd had to have known that he wouldn't have left her if it hadn't been urgent. If he'd only had more time to figure out what had been going on with her. But he'd panicked. He could see that now. After working in an emergency room and with a flight crew, he'd imagined the worst. And he'd been right to.

While the public knew that Nicholas had been involved in an accident, the king had left out the details. Only the medical staff and Alex's father knew that it was touch and go right after the accident.

But that would all end soon. As soon as the crew got up, Summer would be able to see with her own eyes that he had returned just like he had promised her. Then he could explain everything to her, and they could get back to their normal lives together.

After months of living in a palace, he craved his normal life. He needed his normal life.

A dramatic sigh reminded him that his brother was still on the phone. It made Alex want to roll his eyes like a teenager as he made his way down the hall to his office. Both his brother and his father had a flair for drama. "You know the local media has been asking questions about our friendship for years," Nicholas said. "And that little man from the local tabloid, the one that ran all the old headlines about your mother and my father—security caught him sneaking around the service entrance yesterday questioning the staff."

Alex knew the man he was talking about. He'd tried to corner Alex more than once. But Soura and the journalist were far away now. No one would have followed him back to Key West.

"How's the new nurse?" Alex asked. They'd both said everything there was to say on the subject of the king claiming him as his son. They would never agree.

And they didn't need to. It was Alex's life, something he had reminded his father and brother a thousand times in the last few months.

"The woman is a tyrant. Telling me what to eat. When to sleep," Nicholas complained. "Did you really give her an order that I couldn't stay up past midnight?"

"No. I told her you were to get plenty of sleep while you recuperated. I left the rest up to her." Alex had known the moment he'd met the woman that she would be capable of keeping Nicholas in line with the regimen that was needed for his full recovery.

His phone went off with an alert. The crew was being activated.

"Tell the king that I will call soon and don't give Ellie a hard time." Alex could still hear his brother grumbling as he ended the call and took his seat behind his desk only a second before people began to emerge from the sleep rooms that opened into the hallway.

"Boss, you finally found your way home. It's about time," Casey, the first to see him, said, giving him a big smile and wave before he hurried off down the hall.

It was then that he saw her. Standing in the hallway, Summer went from half-asleep to fully awake in a nanosecond. Her eyes met his for only a second before she turned away from him. In that brief moment, he'd seen none of the pleasure he'd hoped for. Instead, there'd been nothing. Not even anger. He could deal with anger. They could talk their way through that. But nothing? He would rather she had yelled at him.

Of course, she was working. It wasn't like she would want to get into things here at work. Especially before she went on a call.

He rubbed his aching head again. He needed sleep, but he needed to talk to Summer more. He turned on his computer and opened up his emails. He might as well get some work done while he waited for her to return.

She'd run. She'd run like a little kid caught with a hand in the cookie jar.

No. More like a scared, embarrassed teenager caught stealing a prom dress at the local department store. Her face heated with the memory.

"You know you're going to have to talk to him at some point," Casey said as they buckled into their seats as their pilot, Roy, started the helicopter rotors. Her queasy stomach did a small somersault as they rose into the air and headed for their small island hospital.

Choosing to ignore him, Summer opened the respiratory supply box. All the adult-size emergency equipment needed to be changed to pediatric size for the little girl they would be transporting to the children's hospital in Miami. "Can you hand me a pediatric IV start kit?"

Casey pulled open the drawer holding the intravenous supplies. "You can't put it off. It's not like he's not going to notice. He's not blind. The two of you just need to talk it out."

She wanted to tell the man that he was not one to give love advice, since he couldn't see what was right in front of his own eyes. But that would mean betraying her friend Jo's confidence and she wouldn't do that, though it was a big temptation. She knew Casey wasn't going to quit dogging her about Alex.

"ETA, two minutes," Roy's voice said over their headphones.

"I'm just saying, Alex will do the right thing," Casey said, handing the supplies over to her.

The right thing? The right thing like her father had done by marrying her mother when he'd found out she was pregnant with her? Would he be doing "the right thing" like her father had done when he'd then left her mother when things got hard? She didn't need anyone else to do the right thing for her. She'd learned at an early age that the only person she could count on was herself. She'd forgotten that for a short period of time while she'd been with Alex. She wouldn't forget it again.

Her hand went protectively to her stomach. No, she wasn't going to let history repeat itself with her. The only thing she needed was to finish this shift and get home before she had to confront Alex at the office. That wasn't the place, and today, when she was worn out from working, wasn't the time.

Casey was right. They would have to talk, but she knew she needed to prepare herself. Just that one look at Alex had made her want to forget the last five months. But that sounded just like something her mother would have done.

She had never been like her mother and she wouldn't let herself become like her. Summer was responsible for more than just herself now. She would continue her relationship with Alex, but it would be with her in the lead. Alex could choose to follow or not. That was up to him.

Today, she had a job to do, and that job was what she needed to concentrate on, not the fact that Alex had finally returned.

Upon arrival, the trauma room they were directed to was buzzing with activity as nurses and the emergency doctor surrounded their patient. Casey moved to talk to the respiratory tech, who was standing by the ventilator that the small child had been attached to.

"What happened?" Summer asked the charge nurse, who was busy filling out the transport paperwork.

"It appears to have been a freak accident. The Fraziers..." The woman motioned to a corner, where a woman and man stood staring at the small, still body of the little girl lying on the oversize trauma stretcher. It was clear that the two of them were in shock. "The Fraziers," she began again, "just arrived from Texas last night. They're staying at a small bungalow with a loft, which is where Emma was sleeping. They think she was trying to get down the stairs and tripped on one of the steps. They called 911 as soon as it happened."

"How bad is it?" Summer asked, having no doubt that the injury had to be more than a broken arm or leg, since Emma had been intubated and needed to be flown off the island.

"Head bleed, fractured skull with a subdural hematoma. Dr. Wade has spoken with a pediatric neurologist in Miami and it was suggested that we go ahead and intubate her before transport. You'll be taking her to the emergency room before she heads to surgery."

Summer saw that Casey and the staff were

about to transfer the child to their own transport stretcher, so she thanked the nurse and moved over to the child's parents.

"My name is Summer, and that," she said, pointing to her blond coworker, "is Casey. We'll be transporting Emma to the emergency room of the children's hospital in Miami. The staff here will give you directions and provide the address. If you give me your number, I'll call you as soon as we arrive and I'll pass your number to the emergency-room staff. Do you have any questions for me?"

"I... W-we don't..." the girl's mother stammered. Her husband wrapped his arm around the woman, who had begun to shake.

"We'll find our way," he said, then pulled a business card out of his wallet, "but if you could please keep us informed?"

Summer nodded, took the card and then stuck it into one of the many pockets of her flight suit. A small hand grabbed her sleeve.

"Please—please take care of my baby," Emma's mother begged as her eyes filled with tears. "And if she wakes up, please tell her Mommy and Daddy love her."

Summer stared into the heartbroken woman's eyes. She couldn't imagine a parent entrusting their child, their world, into the care of someone else. Summer covered the woman's hand with her own and held it tight. "I promise, we'll take the best of care of your daughter."

Summer grabbed the back of the stretcher and followed Casey out of the emergency room, never taking her eyes off the little girl until she was loaded, and the doors were closed.

"Roy, let's make this a fast one," Summer told their pilot, though she knew he always made their trips to Miami as fast and safe as possible.

"Vital signs stable," Casey said as he removed the Ambu bag he'd been using to help the little girl breathe and changed her to their portable in-flight ventilator. "Cute kid."

Summer applied monitor pads and checked the little girl's heart rhythm. "She's still in a sinus rhythm."

"The parents looked freaked out. I hope they make it to the hospital okay," Casey said as he picked up the computer pad to record the events of the transfer.

"Emma's father seems to have a cool head. He'll get them there." The man had impressed her as someone who would do whatever it took to take care of his family.

"It really sucks that something like this happened when they're so far away from home, where they don't know anyone." Casey said.

"It does," Summer agreed as she carefully brushed the little girl's dark hair from her face. She'd spent most of her own life not having anyone she could depend on to help her when she needed someone. "I'll see what we can do to help when I call them from the hospital."

"That sounds like a good plan. I know some of the staff at the hospital will want to help, too. If you can find out the address where they were staying, I can work on getting their things packed up and sent to the hospital. They're not going to leave the hospital long enough to drive back to Key West," Casey said.

"I'll check with them, but I'm sure you're right," Summer said. Casey might be an interfering busybody, but Summer had never met anyone more willing to help someone out when they were down.

"ETA, five minutes," Roy called over the radio.

As Casey used the radio system to call his report into the Miami hospital, Summer checked all the monitors. Emma's vital signs had remained stable throughout the transfer. It was a good sign.

As the helicopter started descending, Summer bent down to the little girl and whispered into her ear, "It's going to be okay, Emma. You're a very lucky girl who has a mommy and daddy that love you very much, and when you wake up, they're going to be right there waiting for you. You just hang on."

The sun was up by the time they made the return trip to the island and a fresh-looking crew met them at the door. Summer was glad to see that Alex's office door was shut when she grabbed her bag from the sleep room.

She was too tired and confused to process all the emotions that Alex's return had brought. Relief? Fear? Pain? Excitement?

No. It wasn't excitement. It was just that she was anxious now that she knew she'd have to face him. She needed to rest and think about exactly what she wanted to do next. There was a time when she would have been happy just to empty out everything she was feeling on Alex. How angry she was. How much he had hurt her. Everything. But that was before. Now her life with Alex would always be divided into two parts. The old part of their life, before he'd left, and the new part of their life, when he had returned. Right now, she wasn't up to dealing with either one. All she wanted to do was go home and climb into her bed.

And if she shed a few tears for that old part of their life, at least there wouldn't be anyone there to see them. Just like there hadn't been anyone to see them the day her worse nightmare had come true. How a day could take you from hope to despair so quickly, she had never understood.

She'd been so excited that morning. Scared, yes, but still excited. She'd known something was wrong for a few weeks. She'd had queasy mornings and her appetite had been off, but she'd blamed it on a stomach bug and gone on with her busy life. It wasn't until she'd begun counting out weeks on her calendar that she'd realized it could be something a lot more serious. One home pregnancy test later and her life had changed.

She'd started to panic. Pregnancy had not been in her plans. Not yet. And Alex? They'd never discussed having children. Only the knowledge that she wouldn't be alone, that Alex would be there with her, had helped calm her fears and bring her hope.

She'd rushed over to Alex's house to tell him, wanting to share the news with him, praying that he would be just as excited as she was, only to find him packing to leave.

"I have to go. A friend needs me," he'd said when she'd questioned him, trying to understand what was happening.

But she could still remember the way he'd pushed past her as he'd headed to his front door, still refusing to explain where or why he had to leave that very minute. Even when she'd known there was something wrong with his excuses, she'd tried to tell him her news. Their news. But he wouldn't stop. He couldn't even give her a moment of his time.

"It's going to be okay. I'll call once I get settled. You can tell me whatever it is then," he'd said, brushing her off as a car horn honked in the driveway. He'd turned and walked away from her carrying a lone duffel bag, leaving her alone and confused.

Until that day she had thought the pain of her father walking away from her had been the worst moment of her life. She'd been wrong.

Alex watched as Summer's car pulled from the parking lot. He'd stayed at the office so that he could see her, and she'd still managed to slip away.

"You know we'll do everything here that we can do. We're family here. This is our home.

We have a great relationship with this community. I'm sure the county board will take that into consideration." Over the phone, the voice of his boss droned on about the importance of Alex's crew at Key West keeping their contract as the door to the office opened.

"I'll send out an email to all the staff," Alex said as he nodded to Casey to come in and take a seat. "Let me know if there is anything I can do to help from here. I'd be happy to meet with the board and answer any questions."

Finally, the phone call ended. If the pain in Alex's head got any worse, he was sure his skull would explode like a volcano erupting. He'd not made a dent in his emails before his phone rang with the call from his boss. This was really turning out to be some welcome-home party.

"What's up?" Casey asked.

Alex pushed away from the desk, stood and walked over to where a picture of their crew, all dressed in their flight suits, hung. They were a great group of caring and hard-working professionals that helped save lives daily. And now they would have to depend on some corporate suits to negotiate to keep their jobs.

"I might as well tell you—I'll be sending out an email today informing everyone that another company is vying for the county emergency-services contract, which will include emergency-helicopter services," Alex said.

Alex's eyes rested on the woman standing beside him in the picture. Standing just barely past his shoulders, her blue eyes sparkled, and her smile shone brightly as she'd posed with the crew for the picture. It hadn't been long after it was taken that he had finally gotten up the nerve to ask her out. Never would he have imagined that things between the two of them could have become this broken.

He'd planned on talking to her the moment she had returned from Miami, but it seemed like phone calls were always coming between the two of them.

First, it had been the call he'd received from his father. Then there'd been those phone calls that Summer had refused to answer. And now, when he had finally made it home, he'd been stopped from speaking to her by another phone call.

"Do you know where Summer was rushing off to?" he asked, hoping maybe she'd said something to Casey concerning her plans.

"I'm pretty sure she was headed home. She worked extra this week and was tired," Casey said. "Should we be worried about this contract business?"

Alex turned away from the picture. He

needed to concentrate on his job, not his relationship with Summer. They'd work things out now that he was back.

"Heli-Care was the first medevac company here in the Florida Keys and we have a great relationship with the community, but the corporate office is taking it seriously. That's their job. We just need to keep giving the best care possible. That's our job."

"And we do it well," Casey said as he stood. "It's a good thing you came back when you did."

"She's pretty mad, I guess?" Alex asked as they both stared at the picture.

"It'll be okay. You both just need to talk," Casey said as he moved toward the door. "I've got faith in you. Just be yourself. You'll know what to do."

Be himself? If only people knew how hard that was for him.

As soon as Casey exited, Alex pulled out his phone and called Summer. If he was lucky, he'd be able to catch her before she went to bed. When the call went to voice mail, he left the same message he'd left for the past five months. "Hey, Summer. Please call me back. We need to talk."

He'd give her some time—she'd had a busy

shift and she would need to recover—but eventually she would have to stop avoiding him. They would talk and it would be soon.

CHAPTER TWO

HER HANDS TIGHTENED on the steering wheel as the large gates leading to Alex's driveway slowly swung open. Though very impressive, with their swirling scrolls of wrought iron, she'd never understood why Alex had had the security gates installed when he'd had the house built. This was Key West, not Hollywood. Of course, she couldn't imagine the lifestyle Alex had lived with his mother in California, where people like them often had to live their lives behind fences.

Maybe that had been one of their problems. They'd come from such different backgrounds. He'd grown up the son of one of the nation's most popular actresses, while she'd grown up in poverty in a small town in Texas.

Why had she ever thought that what the two of them had was more than a fling? People that came from Alex's background didn't mix, for long, with people like her.

No. That wasn't fair. She couldn't compare him to the people in her hometown. Alex had never acted like she didn't belong here. He treated every one of their crew members equally. It was one of the things about him that had first gotten her attention. Well, that and the fact that just looking at him had made her knees go weak.

She had punched the numbers into the gate's keypad, surprised that she remembered the code to get inside the property, though Alex might change it now that they were just... What were they supposed to be now? They'd been friends. Then lovers. And now? Well, that was what she was here to figure out, wasn't it?

She eased her small compact down the crushed-rock driveway with a speed that a conch snail could match. There was no getting around this. She had to face him eventually.

And it had to be on her terms. It all had to be on her terms. It was her life. Her family. She'd lay out everything for him and then explain how things were going to be.

She hit the brakes. She wasn't ready for this. It had sounded so simple in her mind before she had left her apartment, but just the one look at the man yesterday had sent her into a tailspin. His dark brown eyes so intense as they met hers, that day-old stubble that had once scratched her cheek as he'd held her, the dark brown hair that she'd clung to as he'd driven into her body... It had all been too much. Her mind had been filled with memories and her body had turned traitor. She hadn't been able to handle a confrontation with him. Not then. Not when her chest had ached with the same pain that had consumed her the moment he'd told her he was leaving with only the lame excuse of an unknown friend needing him.

It had to have been all her hormone changes. That had been the problem. Just stupid hormones that made her heart race and her eyes water.

There was no way that she still had feelings for him. Letting a man waltz in and out of one's life was an emotional suicide that she'd witnessed too many times in her childhood.

She wouldn't let herself turn into her mother.

She took a moment to shore up her tattered courage. Then, with her back straight and her chin up, she continued down the drive. She parked under the royal poinciana tree, which was full of red blooms, that stood beside the front porch.

The two-story yellow-sided house would be the perfect vacation home anywhere else, but in Key West it was just a way of life. *Sun, sand* and *party* were everyone's favorite words here. But Alex had always treated his home as more of a refuge than a party house, only inviting his closest friends into this part of his life. She'd once been part of that group, part of his life. Now, both of their lives were about to change.

As she stepped out of her car, she tried to imagine how they would go on from here. The last few months of separation had proved that Alex didn't need her in his life like she had thought he had. No matter what happened today, they could never go back to the way things had been before. Not that she wanted to. She'd made the mistake of letting someone control her happiness. She wouldn't do it again.

After ringing the doorbell and not receiving an answer, Summer started to leave. His black Jeep was sitting in the driveway, so she was sure he was home. Was he sleeping? The alarm at the front gate should have woken him. Did he know it was her and didn't want to see her?

That thought reminded her of the last time she'd been there when he hadn't had time for her. Well, that was just too bad. He'd just have to make the time to see her now.

Trying the door, she wasn't surprised to find it locked. Alex was never one to take chances. He'd told her once of a fan of his mother's who'd broken into their home just so that she could sit at their dining room table and pretend to be Melanie Leonelli.

She'd wondered at the time what he would think if she'd told him she'd never even had a dining room. The small, rusted trailer she'd grown up in had only a small bar with two mismatched barstools and she couldn't remember a time when both her and her mother had sat there together.

Deciding to check the locks on the French doors that led out to the patio, she walked around the side of the house.

And there he was. With water dripping from every bare inch of his body, Alex strode out of his pool like the Greek god he had always reminded her of. Her eyes followed a stream of water as it ran down his body. Her knees went weak. Once more Alex sent her heart racing, and this time she couldn't even blame it on her hormones. No, not hormones, at least not the pregnancy kind. No, it was the memories that had her body overheating even as a soft breeze blew against her skin. Memories of his strong arms wrapped around her. Memories of his bare skin sliding over her. Memories of his body hard and hot as it moved against hers.

Her breath caught and she took a step toward him even as her brain told her to turn and run.

Alex's intuition kicked in the minute someone stepped into his backyard. His first instinct was to confront them, but he knew he'd be able to handle the interloper better if he was dressed. After grabbing the towel he'd thrown over a chair, he wrapped it around his waist before turning around. Only, it wasn't a stranger he found standing behind him. It was Summer.

The smile that had begun to spread across his face froze. Something wasn't right. There was something different about her. Something very different. Her beautiful suntanned face was pale. Her bright blue eyes had shadows. But it was her new curvy body, the one with the unmistakable baby bump, that immediately got his attention. And held it.

"I don't understand..." he began, as the wheels in his befuddled brain tried to turn. This didn't make sense. How could this be possible?

Well, he knew how. He even knew the answer to when. But why? He'd used protection. They both had. None of this made any sense.

But that didn't matter at this moment. What mattered was that Summer looked as if she was about to drop.

"You need to sit down," Alex said as he crossed the grass to where she was standing, took her arm and led her to a chair. "We both need to sit down."

He took a seat beside her. He'd known that there was something wrong when Summer had become more adamant about knowing where he was going and when he was returning, but he had never imagined this.

"Why didn't you tell me?" he asked. Hadn't she known he'd have returned the minute he'd gotten the news that she was pregnant? Or did she not tell him because...? "Is it mine?"

He wanted to take back the words the moment they'd left his mouth.

"I can't believe you'd ask me that!" The hurt in her voice was quickly replaced by anger. "If that makes you feel better, then sure, I'll tell you that you're not the father and you can go on disappearing whenever it suits you."

She stood, her face as hard as stone, but this stone looked like it was about to crumble any second.

"Wait," he said before she could walk away.

"I'm sorry, I know it's mine. I do. It's just a shock."

"It wouldn't have been a shock if you had been here," Summer said as she eased back into her seat, though she still looked like she could bolt at any moment.

"You cut all contact with me. You wouldn't take my calls, wouldn't return my texts, and all the time you were pregnant with my child? Why, Summer? Why did you do that?"

"Why should I have told you I was pregnant when for all I knew you had run off to another woman?" Summer said, the color now returning to her face. "And quit staring at my stomach."

"Sorry, it's just…" Alex, a man who had seen every type of trauma, every type of illness and injury, suddenly found himself fascinated with the round bump. A baby. Summer was having his baby.

"As far as me running away with someone, you know that isn't true." At least he hoped she did. They'd never discussed their relationship being monogamous. There had been no reason to. Going from friends to lovers had seemed so natural for the two of them, as if it was meant to be. But this change in their relationship didn't feel natural at all.

"You were gone five months, Alex. I didn't

know where you were or why it had been necessary for you to leave. I didn't even know if you were coming back. You just abandoned your life here, so that you could do…what? Help a friend? It only made sense that this 'friend' was someone you cared for more than…the crew."

She didn't say it. Didn't have to. He knew what she thought. She thought he had cared more for his "friend" than he cared for her. And why shouldn't she have? He'd never expressed how he felt about her. He'd never felt the need to. He'd been taking things slow between the two of them because that's what he did. He didn't jump into things, especially relationships.

His mother said he had trust issues and maybe he did. He'd been burned enough times by people who acted like they were interested in him when all they really wanted was to be close to the Hollywood life he'd been forced to live.

"You should get dressed so that we can talk," Summer said.

He realized then that she'd been waiting for him to say something. To deny her accusations. But what could he say now that she would believe? "It wasn't like that. I was needed there."

"Just get dressed," Summer said, turning her face away from him, as if she couldn't stand the sight of him.

"It's a little late to be worried about my state of undress, don't you think?" Alex said, though he made sure the towel covered him as he stood. They both needed to be at their best for the rest of this conversation. Life had suddenly done a one-eighty and his brain needed to catch up fast. "I'll be back in a few minutes. Don't leave."

His mind raced as he grabbed the first shirt and pair of jeans he found in his closet. He couldn't get past the moment that he'd seen Summer standing there, so beautiful, and so pregnant. Did she have any idea how that had hit him? She seemed so different, so detached from him. So unlike the Summer he'd known.

Going to the kitchen, he studied his fridge and decided on a bottle of water for each of them, though it was tempting to get himself something stronger.

"I think we should have the wedding soon. Something small, if you'd like. Just our friends," he said as he stepped back onto the patio, then handed her the water.

"You think? Excuse me, did I ask you what you thought?" Summer said as she straightened in her chair, her face taut with an anger that should have come with its own warning sign. He'd taken a step in the wrong direction, and he'd better find his way back soon.

"I'm sorry, I just assumed you'd want a smaller affair, but we can do whatever you'd like," Alex said as he sat beside her. He would have to contact his mother. The woman had been hounding him for grandchildren for years.

"It's so nice of you to let me determine how I will change my whole life for you, but I can see we have a terrible misunderstanding. There isn't going to be a wedding," Summer said, her words clipped.

The fact that history was repeating itself was not lost on him. His mother and father had once been in this situation, only then there had been a whole country to think of, something that had made the decision for them both.

But that wasn't the case here. He had no such responsibilities. He only had himself and Summer and their child to think of. And he would do the right thing for his child.

"I understand that this might not have been our plan, but—"

"Not our plan? Of course, this wasn't our plan. Do you think I did this on purpose?" Summer stood and moved away from him, her hand going protectively over her stomach.

"I never thought you did. This is just all a surprise." Alex got up and walked to her. He was messing this up, making things worse, and he didn't know how to stop. Every word he said seemed to be wrong. Why couldn't they just go back to the way things had been between them before he'd left? There had been none of this awkwardness then. They'd been able to talk out everything together.

"Oh, there's a bigger surprise," Summer said. "A lot more. As in a whole-other-baby more."

His eyes went to the prominent baby bump. Another baby? As in two?

"Twins?" Alex asked. Was that squeaky cartoon voice his?

"Yes. Twins. One boy, one girl," Summer said.

Alex noticed the way she smiled, all anger gone, as she rubbed the spot where her— their—babies were. It was the first time she'd smiled since she'd arrived. And this wasn't just a normal Summer smile, though he'd always thought of those as magical. This smile was filled with love and pride.

"None of this would have been a surprise if you hadn't just up and left," Summer said, "and stop staring at my stomach."

"Sorry," he said. He forced his eyes away

from the evidence that their lives were about to change, but it wasn't easy. It was just so fascinating to think that there were two lives inside her that the two of them had made.

And it was scary at the same time. What did he know about being a father? He'd never truly had one. But it wasn't going to be that way for his children. He'd be ever-present in their lives.

"I tried to explain I had no choice." He knew his frustration was spilling out. He'd wanted to tell Summer about his family, his secret family, but he'd wanted to wait until he'd returned home. Or so he'd told himself. Hiding who he was had been ingrained so deep inside him, he wasn't sure if he would have told her then. At least not until a time had come when he'd had no choice.

"And I tried to tell you about the pregnancy, but you were in too much of a hurry," she said.

"You knew then and didn't tell me?"

"I tried. You were too busy rushing off to help your friend to stop and listen to me."

It hit him like a punch in the stomach. If he'd known, if he'd taken a few moments to find out what was so important, everything could have been different. "I'm sorry. I didn't realize."

"It doesn't really matter now, does it?" Summer said, turning away from him.

But it was plain to see that it did. He'd hurt her and though that hadn't been his intention, he knew now he'd been wrong. He should have taken the time to tell her what was really happening the moment he'd received the call from his father. But he'd been totally consumed with getting to his brother and he hadn't had the time he needed to deal with it.

But would he have told her the truth if he'd had the time? He didn't know, not for sure, but he was certain he had to tell her now, before she walked away from him.

"Can we both just sit and talk while I try to explain why I had to leave the way I did?" Alex asked.

He released the breath he hadn't known he'd been holding as she took a seat.

It had been hammered into his head as a young child that he couldn't tell this secret to anyone. When he was young, it had seemed like an adventure to have this big secret that he only shared with his mother and father, and later, his younger brother.

But as he'd gotten older, reality had set in, and he'd realized he wasn't sharing the secret. He was the secret. The secret illegitimate son of a king that would not—or, until recently, could not—claim him.

But this was Summer. And she was going to be the mother of his children. She had more than a right to know. This wasn't just about him anymore. His children's lives, and Summer's, would be changed if the world found out about his parentage. He'd hidden out in Key West without any of the attention he would have received in New York and California from the media. If it came out who his father was, all of their privacy would be gone. He had to trust that Summer would understand that.

He sat down beside her again, then began, "I'm sorry that I didn't explain to you why I had to leave. It wasn't because I was hiding something—there are just some things in my life that I've never been free to discuss with anyone." He stopped and took a swallow of water, then picked up his phone from the side table, where he had left it. "You might know my mother was born in Tuscany, but what most people don't know is that her family moved when her father was assigned to the Italian embassy in Soura."

"Soura? The country where Prince Nicholas is from?" Summer asked.

"We'll get to him later, but yes. Nicholas is Prince of Soura," Alex answered. He should have known that she, like most of the women of the world, had heard of Soura's most eligible bachelor. His brother was always in the media. The attention was something that he seemed to thrive on, something that Alex would never understand.

"Soura's a small but powerful country due to its ports on the Mediterranean Sea. My mother says she fell in love with the country the day she arrived. A few years later, she met my father, the future King of Soura."

"Wait...what?" Summer asked. "I don't understand."

"It's a secret that's been hidden all my life. That's why I couldn't tell you where I was going. Summer, I'm the illegitimate son of King Christos, King of Soura, also known as Prince Nicholas's friend, Alexandro Michael Leonelli—" he handed her his phone "—and if the media ever gets wind of it, I will be hounded by the paparazzi for the rest of my life."

Summer stood up on shaky legs as she looked at the picture of two men standing together beside a large fireplace. She recognized the tall man standing on the left. He had a face that had graced the cover of many gossip magazines. It was the other man that she almost didn't recognize. Dressed in a tailored three-piece suit, the man stood ramrod-straight. His hair had been combed back in a sleek modern style and his face had been shaved meticulously, but none of it fooled Summer. She'd recognize those smoky brown eyes anywhere.

This was a joke. It had to be. Alex couldn't be the son of a king and have never told her. It didn't make sense.

But did it? He'd been only too happy to rush out the door without sharing where he was going with her. Why wouldn't she believe he'd hidden who he was from her, too?

"You're a prince," Summer said as she studied the picture.

It was such a handsome face. An honest face. Or so she had thought. She'd never imagined he was hiding such a big secret from her. But why? Why couldn't he have told her? If he'd planned for the two of them to have any future together, he would have. Wouldn't he? But if she was just a passing fling? No, he wouldn't have admitted anything then.

The fact that he hadn't been honest with her told her so much.

"I can see it. You and Prince Nicholas—you both have the same eyes. And the cheekbones, though his are a bit more angular," Summer said, staring at him for just a moment more before dropping her hand. She got up and quickly backed away from him. "And my babies? What does that mean for them, Alex?"

"This doesn't make a difference. They'll be our children. Both of ours. We'll protect them from all of this," Alex said. He stood now and approached her.

Her hands trembled when he took them into his. "I'm sorry I didn't tell you before. I should have. In a perfect world I would be able to tell everyone who my parents are and then go on with my life, but this isn't a perfect world."

"The news said Prince Nicholas, your brother, had a skiing accident." It made sense now. "That's why you left."

"My father wanted me to oversee Nicki's care," Alex said. "His injuries were worse than what was released to the media."

"This is all too crazy to believe," Summer said, her voice strained. She'd begun to believe that her rural Texas upbringing, when compared to Alex's Hollywood lifestyle as the son of a movie star, didn't matter. But now, to learn he was a prince?

No wonder he had never shared this information with her. She was so out of her depth that he didn't think it was necessary. Her importance in his world of wealth and power was very small, something he had proven when he'd left.

But what if Alex, or this king, wanted to fight her for custody of her babies? Between the two of them, they had more money than she would earn in a lifetime. Maybe she should get a lawyer now. But that took money, and she was going to be on a tight budget with two babies to take care of.

"I can see that it might take some time to process..." Alex began.

"You can't even imagine." She took another step back. "I'm still trying to process the fact that I'm going to be a mother. To twins. And then you tell me that you're this king's son. Oh, but not before you ask me if they are even yours, like I'm some woman that just jumps from man to man." She wouldn't let him see how much that question had hurt her. "And don't forget about your great proclamation that we are to get married as soon as possible."

She could hear the panic in her voice. She needed to leave before she lost it in front of Alex. She wouldn't let him see how much he'd hurt her.

She turned her back to him and started across the yard, but then she whipped back around. "Let's get something straight right now. I'm carrying these babies and for now I will be making all the decisions that concern them. Not you. Not some king. The three of us were doing just fine before you came back.

"No," she said as he opened his mouth to speak. "I've heard enough. I need some time to think."

With her head up, she turned and headed back to her car. She wasn't running away, she was just making a fast retreat so that she could shore up all her defenses in order to protect not only her children, but also her heart. Because though she'd never admit it to Alex, the idea of him asking her to marry him had once been all she had ever dreamed of. It was too bad it had come a few months too late and for all the wrong reasons.

CHAPTER THREE

A FLOCK OF seagulls circled over Summer's head, much like the crazy questions that were turning over and over in her mind.

She'd thought she'd known Alex. His likes, his dislikes. His favorite foods, his favorite sports. He loved a good steak, rare with butter, but he didn't care for roast. He didn't care for hockey, but he watched golf as if it was a religion. He said his favorite color was the blue that matched her eyes. She'd known he was joking, but it had been sweet of him to say it.

Alex had always been sweet, almost perfect; the perfect boss, friend, boyfriend. Until he'd left without telling her the truth, or at least not all of it. She'd known he was holding something back by the way he'd packed so recklessly. Been so unfocused. If only he'd told her the truth. If only he'd shared with her his secret past. And why hadn't he? Because he had never had a reason to. He never would have told her if it wasn't for the babies she was carrying.

And that hurt more than she wanted to admit.

She'd grown up in a town where she'd never been good enough. She'd been the poor kid, the troubled kid. Not good enough to be invited to the party the other kids went to. Not good enough for the other parents to want their kids to hang around her.

And now she knew she had never been good enough for a man who was a prince to share his real life with her. Because while she had been dreaming of their happily-ever-after, she'd just been another happily-for-now to him.

She opened a leftover bag of bread and broke off a piece, then threw it up, and watched as a bold seagull dived down to catch it. She threw another piece up as high as she could and watched as more birds dived toward her. She'd made it a habit to come feed them on her morning walks on the beach ever since she'd moved to the Keys.

She liked to watch the silly birds as they flew away into the sky with a freedom she had envied most of her life. The freedom to fly far away from all the bullying at school. The freedom to fly far away from a life where she'd had no future. She'd found that freedom when she'd become a flight nurse. She loved the rush of excitement she felt every time the helicopter skids left the ground. Being a flight nurse had been the most important thing in her life, until now. Now she had two little ones she was responsible for, so they would be the most important thing in her life.

Telling Alex about the babies was the right thing to do. She would never keep him out of their lives. But having him question if they were his? Having him insist that they needed to get married just because of the pregnancy? It brought back all her insecurities from her childhood and that was something she couldn't deal with right now.

Because one thing Alex had made clear was that he planned to be involved in their babies' lives. *Their* lives, not just hers, and she was going to have to find a way for the two of them to get along for their babies' sake. But how could she do that when every time she saw him her chest squeezed tight into a knot of regret? And how could she trust her babies' future to this man when everything she thought she had known about him was a lie?

Alex watched as the waves crashed against the shore. After a sleepless night, he'd arrived at the beach early enough to enjoy the last of the sunrise and the calming rhythmic motion of the waves before the crowds showed up. Summer loved her early morning walks on the beach, and in the past, he'd joined her whenever he could. He was hoping he'd have a chance to run in to her today.

He'd messed up. It was just that simple. He, a seasoned trauma doc, had panicked the moment he'd heard the naked fear in his father's voice five months ago. He'd always thought the man was made of steel, not flesh and bone, like everyone else. Something had to have been very wrong if his father, the king, was afraid.

"Come home, Alex. You need to see your brother. He's... It's not good. The doctors aren't sure..." His father's voice had trailed off.

The memory sent cold dread running through Alex's body and he was suddenly back in his bedroom, consumed by fear for his brother, a feeling that he had never known. The doctors weren't sure of what? That his brother would survive? What had his brother done now?

"How bad is it, Father? I need to know..." Alex's voice had trailed off as Summer came into the room. What had she heard? If she'd heard him call the king "Father" he'd have a lot of explaining to do—explaining that he hadn't had time for.

"The doctors are taking him to surgery now. There's some internal bleeding they say needs to be stopped. Both of his legs are broken, but they say it is best to wait until he is more stable to operate on those. This is right, yes?"

It wasn't the broken bones that worried Alex. It was the internal bleeding. He'd seen more than one trauma patient bleed out.

"Alex, I need you here," his father said. "You need to come. Now."

It wasn't the demanding tone of a king that Alex heard in his father's voice. It was the fear of a father. His brother's condition had to be bad.

He headed to his closet and pulled down the first suitcase he found. His room at the palace contained most of the clothes he would need. "I'll take the first flight I can get."

"Michael has taken care of all the arrangements. There's a private jet headed from Miami now and a car is headed to your home," his father said. "I'll see you at the hospital."

Alex hung up and headed back into his room, where Summer was sitting on his bed.

"What's up?" she asked as he threw the suitcase on top of the bed.

"I've got to go." He didn't know whom to call first? His boss? Dylan?

"What do you mean you have to go?"

He sent a short text to Dylan. He'd email his boss as soon as he was on the plane. His boss could wait.

"Alex, what do you mean you have to go? What's going on?" Summer asked.

"I have to go out of town." He'd told Dylan that a friend needed him, and it was vital that he'd known it was important that he stuck to the same story. Besides, as far as everyone knew, Nicholas was just a friend. Just a friend of the family.

"A friend of mine needs me. I have to go," Alex said.

"Who is it? Someone from California?" she asked.

"No. No one you know," Alex answered as he headed to the door.

"How long are you going to be gone?" she asked as she followed him.

Alex didn't have the answer. Days? A week? "I don't know. I'll call and let you know as soon as I can."

"Alex, wait…" Her voice rose, and now he knew it was from panic. He'd been leaving her when she'd needed him the most. "I don't understand any of this. Who is this friend? What aren't you telling me?"

Stopping, he set his suitcase next to the door. He could remember now how she'd looked. Her eyes round, her face pale. He'd known he wasn't being fair to her then. He needed to tell her about his brother. He needed to tell her about his whole family. He should have done it sooner, but everything had been so perfect between them without the weight of his secret life and the complications that came along with it.

"It's going to be okay. I'll be back as soon as I can and I'll tell you all about it then, okay?" He hoped he was right. His brother had to be okay. He reached out for Summer, needing the warmth of her body to drive away the cold that had consumed him since his father's call.

"No, it's not okay," she said as she pushed away from him. "I need to talk to you. It's important."

His phone pinged with a text, and he pulled it out of his pocket. He hit the button next to the door to open the front gates.

"My ride to the airport is here. I've got to go." He bent down to kiss her, but she turned her face away from his, startling him. He should have stopped then. He should have known something was wrong. Instead of pushing her aside, he should have taken a moment and listened to her. But instead, he'd grabbed his suitcase and walked out the door.

His last memory was of Summer standing at the door. There'd been no smile, no wave, just a pale Summer leaning against the door-frame looking at him as if he was someone she didn't know.

He lowered his sunglasses and studied the crowd. Unless she'd changed her routine over the last few months, Summer was here.

He had to find a way to make things right between them. He'd been the little boy with-out a father. He couldn't let that happen to his own children.

Oh, he'd had a father, of course, but that man had lived across the ocean. He wasn't at any of his T-ball games or at any of the other sport events that he'd taken part in as a kid. He wasn't there when he'd won the fourth-grade science fair, or even when he'd been valedic-torian of his high school's graduating class.

And when he did get to visit his father, Alex had spent all of his time with his younger brother while pretending to be just a family friend's son that was there for a summer visit. It was no wonder he had ended up confused about who he was. Only when he'd finally settled on a college major in medicine had he felt like he could be someone other than the pampered son of a Hollywood star, or the bastard son of a king.

He would claim his own children, never give them a reason to think that they weren't loved and wanted. And he wanted to do it as soon as possible. He wanted to be there to help them with every science project. He wanted to be there to show them how to throw their first pitch, though he had to admit his mother had tried with that one. If the tabloids had gotten a picture of the beautiful Melanie Leonelli dressed in cut-off jeans and a Dodgers T-shirt trying to throw a baseball, they would have put it on their front page.

He'd never told his mother how much he'd missed having a regular father. He would have never hurt her by admitting that he had needed more than what she was able to give him. She'd done her best to try to make up for his father not being there. But that hadn't been fair to her.

And it wouldn't be fair to their children to not give them the security of both a mother and a father. He just had to find a way to get Summer to accept him back into her life.

It had finally come to him in the middle of the night, that while his first instinct had been to take care of Summer and the babies, it had been unreasonable to think she would agree. He needed to start small. Let her get used to him being back. Remind her of what they'd had together before he'd left. Then he'd propose an equal partnership. While she went through the pregnancy, he'd be there every step. He would help out with chores, go with her to her obstetric appointments and, of course, he would help out financially. It was a simple plan that was beneficial to them both.

Only Summer wasn't a simple woman. And things between them were…complicated. There were still feelings there, no matter how much Summer wanted to deny it. The attraction between the two of them was strong. He'd felt it the moment he'd seen her again. An instant wave of attraction that had run up his spine, then curled deep inside of him, ready to explode at the slightest touch. They'd both felt that once, but it wasn't the same now.

Summer had made it clear that she didn't need him anymore. And it was his fault. Now it was up to him to find a way to make her see that she did need him. They needed each other. Because no matter how complicated things were between the two of them, the most important thing would be their children.

It was a familiar laugh that had him turning to see Summer coming up behind him.

With her head thrown back as she threw bread crumbs up in the air for the seagulls to catch, it was almost as if the woman was just one of the carefree tourists here for a fun week in the sun. She had a guileless beauty, with her bright blue eyes and sweet, honest smile. That girl-next-door beauty that was so different than the cover-girl models his brother dated. They'd always seemed too perfect-looking to be real. Summer looked real.

"How many times have I told you that you're contributing to the delinquency of these poor birds?" he asked as he approached her, not sure how she was going to take his seeking her out.

"But they're hungry," Summer said as she threw another handful of bread crumbs into the air.

She put her whole body into it, her arms shooting up and her feet almost leaving the ground. Her pale blond hair flew in the wind and her eyes lit up with happiness as the seagulls dived down, catching their bounty and then hovering above her with anticipation. It was such a simple thing, feeding the obnoxious birds, but she found so much pleasure in it. But it wouldn't be much longer before she wouldn't be able to move so freely. Not with her carrying twins.

Twins. He'd stopped trying to wrap his mind around that one somewhere around midnight.

"Sorry, guys, I'm all out," Summer said as she folded an empty bag and stuck it in her beach bag. The seagulls circled a few seconds longer and then flew off to hunt for someone else willing to share a meal. "I told you I needed some time."

"It seems I'm running a few months late already. I need to catch up fast," Alex said.

Summer stopped and studied him, her eyes narrowed and her lips pursed. This was not the same woman who'd been laughing just minutes before. "Just because you're a prince doesn't mean you can set your own rules. You need to respect my wishes."

"You're right. I'm sorry. I should have given you some time. It's just like I said—I'm running behind. I haven't been here for you, and I want to change that."

"And like I said, I was doing just fine before you came back," Summer said. She continued walking down the beach, where the high tide was beginning to crash against the shore.

When she raised a leg to remove one of her sandals, Alex's hand instinctively reached out to steady her. With his hand resting on her hip, his fingers tingled with the need to circle around her and stroke her rounded belly.

What would it be like to feel his babies moving inside of her?

What if his arms wrapped all the way around her? Would she lean into him the way she used to? Arch her back and lean her head back on his shoulder?

"I've got it," Summer said as she pushed away his hand from where it had tightened.

"Sorry," Alex said, reminding his body that he was on a mission to get Summer to talk to him, not go to bed with him. Alex wasn't really surprised that she'd shied away from his touch. What did surprise him was how much it hurt. It had been a long time since he'd let anyone get close enough to hurt him. But having her shrink from his touch just reminded him more of what he'd taken for granted.

And what did that say about him? That he'd been so wrapped up in the drama at the palace that he had put what he and Summer had on hold, and assumed that she would be there waiting for him? Maybe he was the spoiled rich kid his classmates had always said he was.

"How long have you been living two lives?" she asked, turning to him, her eyes studying him with an intensity that made him want to squirm.

"What do you mean?" he asked. When he'd shared his secret life with her, he'd known there would be questions. Questions like this that were uncomfortable. How could he make clear his need to separate the two parts of his life, the way he had?

"Don't avoid the question. I saw the picture and you even referred to yourself by another name. You called yourself 'Alexandro' instead of Alex. It's like you're trying to live two different lives. Alexandro and Alex couldn't be more different."

"It just makes things easier," he said. How did he explain the complicated life he'd created?

"For whom? You can't be happy living that way."

He wasn't. He hadn't been for a long time. But what could he do? It was his life.

"I just don't get it. Your mother is this famous actress living in Los Angeles. No one there would be shocked if she came out and acknowledged that your father was some European king. If anything, it would just make her appear even more glamorous."

"My mother wasn't always a movie star. When she came to Hollywood, she was twenty-two and fresh from drama school. I was only a baby. Unlike most of the people who run away to California to become a star, she got lucky. She found an agent that believed in her and within a year she was going on a callback that ended with her starring in the next year's Academy-Award-winning film."

"But what about your father? He is a king. Lots of kings have children by women that aren't their wives," Summer said, her statement such an innocent one.

"Members of royalty play games just like politicians. They have to consider how their actions will affect their popularity. And when I was born, my father was the crown prince, not the king."

They strolled down the beach, each deep in their own thoughts. Once they'd walked this beach hand in hand. Now there seemed to be miles between them. Miles he'd put between them when he'd left.

If he had just trusted her with his secret, they could be walking with hands entwined right now, making plans for the future of their children. Why couldn't he just learn to trust people? Was he so busy protecting his secret life from others that he couldn't take a chance at having a life of his own?

"When my parents met in college, they'd both known that there was no future for them. My father was a crown prince and was expected to marry for the greater good of his country. My mother had her eyes set on Hollywood. Their romance was meant to be a college fling without any complications. And then I came along."

The ocean breeze sent golden tendrils of her hair dancing around her face. She looked so young and innocent.

"Your mother must have been scared," Summer said, her eyes glued to the ocean, where the gulls had been joined by egrets and the occasional pelican as they flew over the crashing waves.

Was she telling him she had been scared?

"I'm sure she was, but she'd never admit it," Alex said. "My mom's tough. You have to be to survive the movie industry."

"But your father was a future king. He could have fought to take custody of you. I checked. You were born eighteen months before Prince Nicholas. You're the true heir to the throne."

"No, I'm not." It was thoughts like this that scared him the most. "I'm considered a royal bastard. Illegitimate. I have no claim to the throne of Soura, nor do I want one. And my father would never have taken me away from my mother. Just like I would never take our children away from you. Never."

"And I would never let you. Not you. Not your father. Not anyone." Summer's harsh voice and fisted hands left him with no doubt that she would do anything to protect their babies.

"You're not on your own here." How did he tell her he wanted to share every part of his children's lives, including her pregnancy, without scaring her off? Maybe he should start with the apology he owed her. "I'm sorry I wasn't here for you. And I'm sorry I didn't tell you about my family."

"I thought…" she said, then shook her head. "Never mind. It's not important. Yes. You should have told me."

Every man knew that when a woman said that it didn't matter, it really, really mattered. "Still, I'm sorry I let my own…issues come between us."

"And when you came back without an explanation, what did you think would happen? I'd forgive you and fall back into your arms?"

Because that was exactly what he had thought, he kept his mouth shut. He was a bastard in more than one way. He'd truly thought the two of them had all the time in the world until he'd found out their clocks weren't ticking at the same rate. Summer's clock was more than five months ahead of his.

"Well, that's not going to happen. I trusted you and I thought you trusted me, too. It's not like we just jumped into bed one night. We were friends. At least I thought we were."

"We were—are—friends. I'm sorry I hurt you. I was wrong. I shouldn't have left without telling you the whole story."

"You should have told me about your parents a long time before you left," Summer said. "If you had thought we had any type of future together, you should have told me."

"But I want to make things right now. I want to be there for you and the babies. Our babies. We can do this together a lot easier than we can do it separately, don't you think?" Alex asked.

"What I think is that I'm perfectly capable of doing everything by myself, as I have been for the last five months," Summer said.

"I'm not saying that you aren't—" The sound of a woman's scream cut through his words and his body went on high alert. He knew the sound of fear when he heard it. There was no doubt that someone was in trouble.

CHAPTER FOUR

"WHERE?" HE ASKED as he scanned the beach for the woman. Where had that scream come from?

"She's there," Summer said as she started sprinting toward the woman, her steps slowed by the thick sand.

Alex scanned the area where the woman was standing in water up to her chest and then turned his attention to the place where she was staring in horror.

"I see him," he shouted as he rushed into the water and began to swim. The teenage boy was still above the water, but Alex could see he was struggling. He poured more power into his breaststroke. If Alex didn't make it to the kid before he went down, his chances of saving him were slim.

Just ten yards to go. The boy's eyes, wide with fear, met Alex's as he closed in on him.

Alex pushed his arms and legs to maximum

speed, but his limbs began to protest. Just five more yards. Just a couple more strokes. He would make it. He just needed the boy to hang on for a few more seconds. Alex reached out and grabbed for his hand, but his fingers met only water as the boy's body went under.

No. He wouldn't lose this kid. Alec dived down with powerful kicks even as his muscles began to cramp. He grabbed what he hoped was the boy's arm and headed for the surface. He broke through the water and took a badly needed breath, then looked around, quickly locating the beach. A crowd had gathered, and he headed toward land. The limp body in his arms told him he needed to get the boy to the shore fast.

As his muscles strained and cramped, he pushed himself harder, dragging the kid with him as he kept his arm tight across the boy's chest and worked his free arm and his legs until he reached the shallow water, where a man took the boy from Alex's shaking arms.

"Get him onto his back," he said to the man as soon as they made their way onto the sand, as Alex worked to catch his own breath. The fight for this boy's life was not over.

"Emergency services are on their way," Summer said as she went down on her knees beside Alex. Her own heart had seemed like it had stopped when she'd seen Alex go under the water, only restarting with a quick gallop when he'd broken through the surface, hauling the boy up with him.

She'd felt so helpless watching as Alex had risked his own life fighting through the waves to get to the boy. She considered herself a strong swimmer, but she would never have been able to do what Alex had done, even if she wasn't pregnant.

Seeing the boy was nonresponsive when the bystander placed him onto his back, she turned the boy's head to the side to help any water drain out as she watched his chest. After ten seconds with no respirations, she bent over the boy. The kid wasn't breathing, and his pale blue lips told her all she needed to know. There wasn't time to wait for the ambulance.

Pinching his nose, she positioned the young man's head back and placed her lips against his cold lips, then breathed into him. The first breath went in easily, as did the next three. Her hope took a dive when she took another breath and saw that Alex had begun compressions on the boy's bare chest. Total arrest. The kid was barely into puberty. He had too much of life ahead of him.

She gave him another breath and another.

They would get him back. Alex had risked his own life for him. They wouldn't give up.

It seemed like hours; though she knew it had likely been less than fifteen minutes since this nightmare had begun, when she heard the siren and then the welcome pounding of feet as a pair of EMTs joined them.

"I can take over," a young woman said to Summer as she pulled out an Ambu bag from her bag.

Summer had just lifted her head and started to pull away when she saw the boy's chest heave and his stomach muscles clench. As she turned the boy's head, both the EMT and Alex helped roll him onto his side.

Looking over at Alex, Summer grinned as the boy coughed up the water that had almost taken his life, then took his first breath on his own. They'd done it. The kid was still not out of the woods. The complications from nearly drowning could be serious. He'd have to be watched in an intensive-care setting for signs of respiratory complications such as pneumonia, but he was young. His chances of a full recovery were good.

Alex stood and offered her a hand as the EMTs moved in and took over. Looking up at the smile on his face, she took his hand.

And for a moment, as her body warmed and

her heart raced, with her chest pressed against his, it was as if time had turned back. Back to before she'd told him he was to be a father to her twins. Before he had left her. Back to when things between them hadn't been complicated. It was as if they were a team again, working together, playing together and, yes, loving together.

Just two people that enjoyed being together. Carefree with no worries about the future, as both of them were willing to enjoy each day as it came. They'd been falling in love—at least, she had been—but there had been no commitments. They had plenty of time for that. Or so they had thought.

But that was their old life and she needed to put it into the past. She had her babies. They had to be her priority. It was time to move on. And standing here in Alex's arms was not making things any easier.

She pushed back from him, unwilling to admit to even herself how much strength it took when all she wanted to do was lay her head against his strong shoulder and let him take care of her.

And that was exactly what her mother would have done. Let someone take care of her. And she was not her mother. She could take care of herself. She always had.

She took another step back and was suddenly aware that the two of them had become the center of attention, as some of the crowd around them broke out into applause while others had their phones glued not on the EMTs and their patient, but on her and Alex.

"Thank you, thank you," said the woman, whom Summer assumed was the boy's mother, as she threw herself between the two of them, hugging Summer and then Alex.

"You saved my son," the woman said, breaking down in Alex's arms. Alex held her as she cried out her relief. He was always so good with people, dealing with the grief and worry of his patients' families. His empathy for his patients was one of the things that made him a favorite in the local hospital's emergency room.

"How about we drive you to the hospital?" Alex said, as the EMTs transferred her son, still coughing and looking dazed. "We'll follow the ambulance, and you can talk to the doctor."

Summer reached over and put an arm around the woman as the two of them guided her behind the EMTs. "Is there anyone you want us to call for you?"

The dazed woman looked down at her empty hands. "I need to call my husband—

he's in a conference meeting at our hotel, but I left my phone in the car. Can we stop and get it?"

After picking up the woman's phone, Summer helped to explain to the boy's father what had happened and where to meet them at the hospital, while Alex kept up a dialogue of questions meant to keep the woman as calm as possible. The woman's name was Maggie and they'd arrived for her husband's business conference just the day before. She and her son had been amazed at the clear blue color of the water surrounding Key West when they'd flown in the night before, and had made plans to hit the beach early this morning. She couldn't imagine what had happened that her son had been pulled out in the water so quickly. Summer didn't think it was the time to explain the dangerous undercurrents that caught so many visitors off guard, or the fact that there were red flags out warning people of the danger.

As soon as they arrived at the hospital, Summer led the woman to a nearby waiting room while Alex went to find the doctor who would be taking care of the woman's son, Scottie.

"It's good news," Alex said as he rushed into the waiting room. He'd changed into a pair of green hospital scrubs and looked every bit the doctor that he was. "Your son is doing well. He's not requiring any ventilation at this time. He's only on the minimum of oxygen, though you need to be prepared that could change. Because his lungs filled up with water, he could develop aspiration pneumonia, so he'll have to stay in the hospital a few days. But for now, he's stable and he's asking to see you. The nurses said they'll come and get you in as soon as they get him settled."

A man with graying hair hurried into the waiting room, an emergency-room nurse following behind him and offering to take them to see their son. The woman hugged them both once more before leaving the room.

Summer watched the couple leave arm in arm. This could have turned out a different way, Summer thought. They could have been going to say goodbye to their child if it hadn't been for Alex. "You saved that boy's life."

"We save people's lives every day," Alex said.

"But this time was different. You put your own life on the line." And she hadn't liked it one bit. She might have been angry, and hurt by Alex's actions, but she still cared. She cared a lot, and it didn't have anything to do with the children that she was carrying.

She stood, too quickly it seemed, because

the room began to spin, and she felt light-headed. Instinct had her reaching for Alex and his arms went around her.

"What's wrong?" he said, his hand cupping her chin. "You're as pale as a sheet."

She closed her eyes and took a deep breath as she felt the blood rush back into her head. "I just got up too fast. My blood pressure dropped. I'll be fine in a couple of minutes."

She bit her bottom lip as she fought against the nausea that was soon to follow and continued to breathe deeply.

"Have you talked to your doctor? I can call them and we can check you into the emergency room," Alex said, his voice pitched higher than it had been just moments earlier.

The man had just saved a drowning victim and he was panicking over a little case of hypotension?

"No, I do not need to call my doctor. I'm fine. I'm just behind on my fluid intake for the day. We've been a bit busy this morning."

She stood perfectly still as Alex studied her eyes—he was checking her pupils, she was sure. He stood so close to her that she could smell the seawater that still dampened his skin, causing her heart rate to increase to a number that would have Alex admitting her to the hospital if he took her pulse. "I'm telling you I'm fine."

Unable to stand being close to him a second longer, she turned her chin away from him and stepped back. "We need to get back to the beach. I have some water and a granola bar in my car."

Alex didn't say a word as they made their way to the car, and she was glad. It was taking all the energy she had just to get back to the parking lot. After climbing into his truck, she found herself unable to keep her eyes open as he pulled out into traffic. The sleepless night and the excitement from the rescue had caught up with her. She closed her eyes and let the needed sleep take her.

Alex looked over to where Summer was now dozing in his passenger seat. She'd scared him when she'd turned that sickly color between slime-green and ghost-white. And he hadn't even known whom to call. He didn't know the name of the doctor who was taking care of her. What was wrong with him? That should have been one of the first things he'd asked. He needed to know that he was leaving the health of Summer and the babies in good hands. He hadn't even had the sense to ask if there were any complications with her pregnancy. A twin pregnancy could be dangerous. What if she had preeclampsia?

No, she'd said she was hypotensive and with her experience as a nurse he had no reason to doubt that she was aware of what was going on in her own body. Still…he couldn't help but worry.

He parked the truck a couple of blocks from the beach and turned to where Summer was sleeping. Her head leaned against the truck door window, and her long lashes swept down onto cheeks that still looked pale under her golden tan. All her anger at him seemed to be gone for this moment. She looked so innocent and sweet, as she had looked earlier on the beach, but he wasn't fooled. The woman was going to give him the fight of his life before she accepted any help from him. He just had to be ready for it. He could be as stubborn as she was when it came to the lives of his children. His plan had been to take small steps and that was what he would do.

Her eyes fluttered, and then opened. Baby blues stared up at him and his heart turned over in his chest. He loved that look. The one she had when she awoke to find him watching her sleep. The look she'd give him right before she lit up with a mischievous smile and rolled on top of him. With lips and tongues, hands and fingers, she'd given him the best mornings that he had ever had.

"Why are we here?" she asked. There was no smile directed at him now.

"We've had a busy morning. I thought we could both use some food." It would do no good to point out the fact that she was still pale.

Her lips pursed and he waited for her protest. Summer had always been very independent, and he'd admired that. But now it seemed she was even more determined to prove, at least to him, that she didn't need anyone's help.

She turned away from him and climbed out of the truck, leaving him behind as she headed into the open French café.

"Hey, Summer," Kevin, one of the waiters called as he pulled out two menus. "Alex, it's been a while."

"I had to leave town for a few months," Alex said, looking over to Summer, "but I'm back now."

"That's good. We missed you around here," Kevin said. They followed him to a small table set beneath a tree covered in white blossoms. "What can I get you to drink?"

"A small iced coffee would be wonderful," Summer said.

"Make that two and we'll both have a glass

of orange juice, too," Alex said, ignoring the deadly pointed stare Summer gave him.

"If I had wanted juice, I would have ordered it. And I'm allowed one coffee a day," Summer said as soon as the waiter walked away.

"I'm feeling a bit drained after this morning. I thought you might be, too," Alex said. The look of concern she gave him increased his guilt at lying to her, but if the juice helped put some color back into her face, it would be worth it.

"Can I take your picture?" a voice asked from behind him.

Turning, he saw a young girl who couldn't have been over eleven or twelve. Beside her a stood a younger boy. Dread seeped into every pore of his body. It had happened. His father had finally called his bluff and outed him.

"Uh…sure, I guess," Summer said.

Before he could stop her, the young girl pointed her phone at them and clicked the picture before running back over to a table, where two women smiled and waved at him. After waving back with a smile as stiff as a porcupine quill, he quickly turned back to Summer. "We need to get out of here."

He had to make some calls and the first one would be to his traitor brother, who hadn't had the decency to warn him. Because he had to know. Nicholas always knew what social media was saying about the royals of Soura thanks to some app he'd set up to scan the internet. The man would have made quite the IT guy if it wasn't for that pesky royal title.

"What was that about?" she asked.

"My father might have—" Alex stopped as the waiter approached their table.

"How does it feel to be a hero?" Kevin asked as he put their drinks in front of them. "I just saw the video in the kitchen."

"What video?" Summer asked, then took a drink of her coffee.

"Someone posted it to the city's social-media accounts. It looks like the two of you had a busy morning. Jacques says your meal is on us today," Kevin said as he pulled out his order pad. "What will it be?"

As soon as their orders were taken, Alex reached for his phone only to realize it was in the wet shorts he'd thrown into the back seat of his truck when they'd left the hospital. He'd be lucky if it could be saved after the swim he'd taken, even though it was supposed to be waterproof.

"Here," Summer said as she pulled her phone out of her beach bag, "I've got mine."

He waited while she searched. After finding what she was looking for, she moved her chair next to his and started the video playing.

Whoever had taken the video had some major skills with their phone camera as they had zoomed in and captured the moment Alex had dived under the water to save the kid and then resurfaced. Then they'd zoomed out and caught the reaction of the crowd as he'd fought the waves back to shore. But instead of stopping at the rescue, they'd continued filming as he and Summer had worked together to resuscitate the boy, even filming when the poor kid had puked up half the ocean and finally taken a breath. They'd even videoed the moment when he'd helped Summer up and held her until she'd regained her footing.

"Are you feeling uncomfortable with this, or is it just me?" Summer asked. "I mean I'm used to being surrounded by a crowd. But it's just weird watching from the other side."

Alex felt more than uncomfortable. He'd been the subject of too many cameras growing up in Hollywood. It was never as simple as someone taking a picture or filming you. There were always those people that felt they had the right to make comments about your looks, what you were wearing or where you were going. Why couldn't people just mind their own business?

But this wasn't filmed by the paparazzi trying to make a quick buck; this had been done by someone who was just been caught up in the moment. He'd need to remind himself of that as this video made the local rounds.

"Go back a few seconds," Alex said, as he realized the cause of his concern.

Summer tapped the screen, taking the recording back thirty seconds. "Here?"

"Yeah," Alex said as he bent down closer to the phone screen. "Now stop it."

She tapped the screen again, pausing the recording. "What is it?"

The screen showed the two of them working on the patient, but that wasn't what had gotten his attention. "See that man in the back, the one with the black baseball hat?"

"Do you know him?" she asked.

"I think so. If he's who I think he is, he had no business being in Key West." No, the man on the screen should be far away from Key West. He should be in Soura, writing for the local tabloids and causing trouble for Nicholas.

"Who is he?" Summer asked, putting her phone away as their food was delivered.

"He's a journalist who makes his living by searching for smut on all the local royalty and celebrities in my father's country."

Alex dug in to the plate of eggs and ham

while keeping a watchful eye on Summer, making sure that she was eating enough for three. Three. It was crazy to imagine, let alone accept, that the woman sitting next to him was carrying two tiny beings. How was that small body of hers supposed to support all of them?

"But what is he doing here?" Summer asked, before her eyes went wide. "He's here because of you?"

"I'm assuming so, though I don't know what he thinks he's going to find here. No one here knows anything about my relationship to Soura."

"No one but me," Summer said. "Should I be worried?"

"I don't know," Alex said, before going back to his eggs. What could the man want from him? Or was he following some lead that had landed him here? And how long had he been following? He'd been spotted at the palace the day before Alex had left. Had Alex been followed home? If so, the man might have seen Summer enter the grounds of his home. He'd have to call his brother and find out more about the man. Then he'd have to figure out how to handle him. There were times it was nice to have his father's backing. This might be one of those.

"My obstetrician is Dr. Wade. She came

very well recommended," Summer said, surprising him.

It was such a small thing to know—the doctor who would be taking care of her and their twins—but it was the first step in finding his way to take part in Summer's life. "I know her from working in the emergency room. She's very good."

"I'd like to go to the next doctor's visit with you, if that's okay with you." He wouldn't push. Not yet. This would be one of those small steps. Things would go a lot more smoothly if Summer agreed to let him be involved with the pregnancy.

"I'll see," Summer said.

Her noncommittal response was disappointing, but it was a start. Seeking her out today had worked, though he would never have imagined that it would end up with the two of them working together to save a life. But that had been good, too. After all, that was where their relationship had started. But there was one thing that he didn't understand.

"Can I ask you something?" he said.

"You can ask," Summer said, her eyes narrowing with suspicion.

"I just want to know how in the world you managed to keep the whole helicopter crew, *my* crew, quiet about the fact that you were pregnant. That group can't keep quiet about anything," he said.

"I didn't have to do anything. Jo took care of it," Summer said as her lips turned up in a conspiratorial smile. "She claims to know where to hide the bodies."

"I see," he said. Jo could be a bit scary when she wanted to be. And with a six-foot Viking, Casey, as her best friend, it was easy to understand why the rest of the crew might have been intimidated. That and the fact that they respected Summer's privacy.

Summer's phone dinged once, followed quickly by two more alerts. She picked it up and laughed. "Speaking of the crew, it looks like they just saw the video."

She held out the phone to show him a screenshot of their faces on the local news station as she said, "It looks like the two of us are going to be famous for a few hours."

"I better give Corporate a call just in case they see it. Those risk-management people don't like being blindsided," he said.

A half hour later, he dropped off Summer at her car with orders to get some rest, because he knew she only had the one day off before she would be back on duty for a twenty-four-hour shift. When she grumbled back at him, he smiled and waved, pretending he didn't see her stick her tongue out at him.

Did she know how cute she looked with one hip cocked to the side, her hand across her new curvy abdomen? Or was she just trying to goad him?

If so, it was a dangerous game she was playing, because it was taking everything he had not to turn his truck around.

CHAPTER FIVE

ALEX HAD JUST turned onto US Highway 1, heading to Marathon, when his phone rang. He'd already made his dutiful call to Heli-Care's risk-management department. He'd been forwarded to Marketing to go through the whole story again of his and Summer's morning at the beach. The last thing he wanted to do was go over it once more with his boss. He could ignore the call. But after taking so much time off for his brother, he needed to play nice.

"You're a genius," his boss said immediately.

"That's nice to hear," Alex said, "but since I've been out of the office and Dylan was managing the crews, I think he's probably due the compliment."

"I'm talking about the video of you saving the boy. I've already heard from the marketing department that the news channels in Miami are picking up the story. You've been recognized as being the medical chief for the local Heli-Care by someone, and one of the stations has asked to interview you and your crewmate for the news."

The man had no idea what a can of worms an interview could open for him. The last thing he and Summer needed right now was to be put in the spotlight. Not that it sounded like his boss would care.

"I'm not sure that would be a good idea. Neither one of us really want the attention. We were just doing our jobs."

"But you weren't on the job. That's what makes this so appealing to the public. You went beyond what is expected when you dove into the surf to save that kid."

"We'll have to talk about it. Summer is pregnant with twins. This might be too much for her," Alex said as he searched for any way to get out of his boss's plans. Since the video had only been broadcast locally, he'd seen no real threat in it. But to be put on a Miami television stage, where thousands of people could recognize him?

All he wanted was to work in peace while convincing Summer that together they could make a family for their babies. Was that too much to ask for? It must be, because it seemed he'd spent his whole life searching for somewhere he could live in privacy, and he still hadn't found it.

"It will be great coverage to show that Heli-Care is a vital part of the community." As the man went on and on about negotiations with the Monroe County board of commissioners, Alex lost all hope of getting out of the interview. All he could do was hope that Summer was up for it. At least it was just Miami, which was a long way from both Hollywood and Soura.

Summer sat rigidly beside Alex as she waited to be called to the studio stage to be interviewed by the *Good Morning, Miami* hosts. She'd done her best, including threatening to puke on the audience, to get out of this pony show. It hadn't worked. And after attending Alex's staff meeting concerning the possible loss of Heli-Care's contract, she'd understood why. Her crew needed her to step up and represent them this morning. Unfortunately, she was afraid her threat of puking on the audience might come true.

"It's going to be okay," Alex told her, then patted her hand like she was some little old lady in need of comfort.

She pulled her hand away from him. The

last thing she needed was for him to touch her. Between nerves and hormones, she didn't require any more stimulation.

And if he mentioned one more time how pale she looked, he'd be sporting a black eye for the whole television-viewing audience. "I'm fine. Me and Max got called out to help the Marathon crew at that pileup yesterday on Highway One. Five cars. Six injured. One fatality. This is nothing."

She rolled her shoulders and raised her chin. She could do this.

"It's time, guys," a perky redhead with her eyes glued to the tablet in her hand said as she rushed into the room. "Let's go."

The woman herded them onto a stage where Debbie Duncan, Miami's favorite TV host, or so the billboard Summer had passed on the way to the studio stated, was waiting for them.

"Now get comfortable." The platinum blonde with lips painted redder than a crime scene motioned for her to take the outer seat before she turned to Alex.

Dressed in a gray tailored suit that probably cost more than Summer's rent that month, he looked every bit the successful doctor, while it had been requested by Heli-Care's marketing department that Summer wear her flight suit. She felt like some dowdy Cinderella sitting next to His Highness. Summer watched the woman's eyes check out Alex's fingers before she patted the chair next to her. "Dr. Leonelli, you take the chair by me."

Could the woman be any more obvious? Now Summer knew she was going to puke. Except, no. Her queasy stomach had settled down for the moment. Her only problem now was the fireball of anger that wanted to explode outward when their lovely host leaned over, rubbing her chest against Alex's shoulder, and whispered something into his ear.

If that woman thought she was going to get Alex's attention, she was wrong. She wasn't his type.

And Summer knew this how? Her stomach dropped. Just because this woman was as far from Summer as possible didn't mean Alex wouldn't be interested in her. Maybe the doctor had been attracted to her, but it was possible that the prince would want someone from more acceptable circles.

And now her mind was turning to mush. It had to be the pregnancy playing with her normally sensible thoughts. Alex hadn't suddenly changed just because he had admitted to her that he was born of royal blood.

Well, Alex hadn't changed, but what did

she really know about this Alexandro he pretended to be?

A man said something to Debbie and seconds later Summer was hit with a bright light as the studio audience began to clap on cue at the video starring Alex and Summer.

"Let's welcome Dr. Alex Leonelli and Summer Madison, our two local heroes," Debbie Duncan said as she turned her smile toward Alex and the audience clapped again. "Dr. Leonelli, can you tell us exactly what went through your head when you saw that young boy out in the water in trouble?"

"Well, Debbie, I think I thought the same thing anyone here would have thought. The kid needed help. Fortunately, I'm a good swimmer," Alex said, his voice strong.

"And you, Summer? What did you think when you saw your boss diving into the water?"

Summer froze. She couldn't tell them the truth. That for a moment her heart had stopped, and her brain had refused to function. She'd watched him go under and prayed that he would come back to her. But she couldn't tell them that. "Like Alex, I thought what anyone else would have. They needed help so I called 911."

She released the breath she'd been holding

as Debbie turned her attention back to Alex. "I know the two of you work together in the medical field and are used to performing heroic measures, but what did you think when you discovered that someone had not only videoed the rescue, but also that the video had gone viral?"

Alex gave Debbie a smile so bright that Summer wondered if the glare from his white teeth would blind the people watching the show.

"I have to say that we were both surprised. Drowning victims are rescued every day. We just happened to be in the right place that morning," Alex said.

"Well, I have to tell you I had my own surprise after the video went viral and I did some digging and discovered that this wasn't the first time you've been videoed," Debbie Duncan said, her smile just as bright and blinding as Alex's. "And I'm sure our audience will also be surprised to discover that you're the son of one famously gorgeous and talented movie star."

Summer blinked. This had not been on the list of things that they had gone over that might be asked. Her attention went to Alex. If someone didn't know him, all they would be seeing was the same relaxed man that had entered the studio. But Summer knew him. Those brown eyes were guarded now, and his body had become rigid. He had flown under the radar in Key West and now some snoopy reporter was going to change everything.

"My mother would appreciate the compliments, Debbie," he said, his smile never faltering.

Summer waited for the woman to continue to question him about his mother and was surprised when she turned to her instead.

"Summer, we also understand that you have a bit of exciting news. Would you like to share it with our audience today?" Debbie asked, her smile as sweet as Summer's grandma's tea.

"I'm not sure..." Summer's brain raced.

"It seems there was a lot of speculation in the viral-video world that you might be expecting a little one, and when I spoke to Scottie's mother, she let me in on the news that you are expecting not one, but two little ones later this year. She, as we all are, was impressed at the way you worked so hard to save her son. We just wanted to congratulate you." Debbie looked out into the audience as they all began to clap.

Summer remembered now the boy's mom had asked if she was okay as they'd made their way to the car from the beach that day. She'd been surprised at the woman's concern at first, until she'd realized that the T-shirt she'd been wearing had become damp from helping with the drowned boy's resuscitation and was outlining what clearly was her baby bump. As far as any comments on her condition after the video had come out, she hadn't even bothered to read them. It seemed now that had been a mistake.

"Yes, I am expecting twins," Summer said, keeping her answer short in the hope that the show's host would turn her attention back to Alex. Besides, there wasn't any reason for her to deny it and maybe now that this overbearing TV host had spilled everyone's secrets they could end this interview.

"And still, as we all saw in the video, you worked so hard to help save this young man. The father of those babies must be very proud of you," Debbie said, her smile still in place, though her eyes had narrowed into a beam of interest that Summer didn't like.

Summer had agreed to be interviewed for the good of Heli-Care, not to be hunted by a rabid journalist that smelled a story where there shouldn't have been one. But there was a story. A big juicy one that would shoot this woman's career up a notch if she ever learned about Alex being of royal blood. Or, more importantly, of Summer's twins being of royal blood.

Summer opened her mouth to respond, but nothing came out. She needed to say something. Something noncommittal that would stop Debbie's questions.

"Of course, I am," Alex said as his warm fingers covered hers where they rested on her chair.

Her eyes darted up to his in shock. Though there was no doubt their close friends knew that Alex was the father of her babies, there had been no conversation about how they would announce this.

And now, Alex basically had announced it to the world. Their local world, but still, this should have been something that they discussed first.

As the crowd once more gave them a round of applause, Summer looked back at the host. There was still something in the woman's eyes that made her uncomfortable. This woman wasn't done. For some reason, she had taken a professional, or personal, interest. Maybe it was just the glamour of Alex's Hollywood upbringing that had caught the woman's attention. Or maybe it was just the woman's physical attraction to the hot-doc image of Alex that Summer had seen over the years.

But whatever it was, Summer knew they hadn't seen the last of Debbie Duncan.

How she had made it through the rest of the show without losing it, Summer didn't know. But the moment the two of them stepped into the studio parking lot, she exploded. "Why did you do that?"

"What?" Alex asked, as if he didn't know what she could be upset about.

"Don't play dumb. You knew from the moment you opened your mouth that what you were doing was wrong." It was more likely that he had done it on purpose. "You should never have announced something like that to anyone, let alone the entire Miami population, without talking to me first. And what about that man that was following you? Did you stop and think about him? What if he saw the show?"

Alex scrubbed his hand over his face before he looked back at her. "I'm sorry. It just seemed as if that woman had you cornered."

It was true. Debbie had cornered her with the question. The woman must have suspected that there was something between the two of them. "Maybe she did, but you should have given me the opportunity to answer. I thought we had an understanding, but I guess I was wrong."

"They're my children, too, Summer. I couldn't sit there and not claim them."

And just that quickly, she realized what had happened. Alex had truly done what his father had never done. He'd claimed his children and had thousands of witnesses to the act. Not that it made what he had done okay.

She reluctantly climbed into Alex's car when he opened the door for her. For a man who could be so empathetic, he showed no signs of appreciating her feelings at being robbed of the decisions concerning her life and those of her children. If they were going to make co-parenting work, she had to find a way to make him understand.

She waited until he'd buckled himself into the car before turning toward him. "And if I had decided that since they are my children I should announce their royal heritage, that their father was really a prince in hiding, would that have been okay with you?"

His hands on the steering wheel stilled, but he didn't turn toward her. She'd known she was cutting open a wound that he denied existed, but she had to make a stand. It was better to do it now, rather than after the babies were born.

"Okay, I get it. I won't do or say anything about the babies before I get your permission," Alex said, though he still seemed a little too proud of himself. The man might deny that he was royalty, but he sure did act like it.

"Let's be clear. If you ever do anything like that again, make any decisions concerning these babies without talking to me first, I swear I'll get a lawyer involved. That's not what I want, but I'll do it."

Finally, he looked at her, the shock on his face telling her that she had hit her target right in the heart. Guilt flooded her, but she pushed it away. It hadn't been her goal to hurt him. All she had wanted was for him to understand how she felt about her own feelings not being considered.

The ride back to the Keys was long and uncomfortably silent. She rubbed her belly as one of the infants did a somersault with all four limbs jabbing her belly while she fumed about what Alex had done. She had thrown up a wall between them and she didn't know if she should leave it, or try to break through. Right now, leaving it between them seemed to be the best option.

She was sure Alex had grown up getting everything he had ever wanted. It was time for him to learn that it didn't always work that way. If he wanted to work with her, fine. But if he thought he was going to be in charge of their children's lives, she would have to show him just how wrong he was. And if that meant bringing in a third party, she would do it. She didn't want to, but she would. Because no one, not even the Prince of Soura, was going to be making decisions about these babies without her.

CHAPTER SIX

"I JUST TURNED my back for a moment," the young mother said as she ran her hand across her little girl's hair. "It happened so fast."

"It looks like she took a pretty good whack to the head," Alex said as he looked at the cut across the three-year-old's forehead, "but the CAT scan doesn't show a fracture. I'm just going to use a special glue to close this up. She's going to have a nasty-looking bruise, but just keep the cut clean and dry and she'll be fine."

"And you, Miss Valeria—swings are made to be sat in, not to get hit by." Unable to help himself, Alex brushed away the little girl's tears, then started to apply the bandage glue to the cut. "I bet as soon as we get your boo-boo taken care of, I can find you a lollipop. Do you have a favorite color you want?"

The little girl's wiggling stopped as Alex's

offer got her attention. "I like red lollipops. Bubba likes red, too."

"In that case, we'll make it two lollipops," Alex said as he finished checking the cut and making sure the sides were approximated.

A few minutes later, after delivering on his promise of two lollipops, Alex left the room feeling like a real doctor for the first time in a long time.

He loved his work with Heli-Care, but he needed to spend this time working with the everyday injuries and complaints of the patients that came in for treatment when they had nowhere else to go, especially after-hours, when the physician offices were closed for the night.

"Just got a call from the Heli-Care crew. They're bringing in a chest-pain patient. ETA, three minutes."

"Thanks," he told the unit coordinator before taking a seat at his desk. Summer was flying tonight with Jo, so he knew the patient was in the best of hands.

It had been two days since he had seen Summer. Two days of waiting for her to get over being mad at him for, quote "proclaiming to the world that you're the father of these babies." And, yes, it had brought him a lot of pleasure to make that announcement. Why shouldn't it have? He was going to be a father of two little babies that had already won his heart even though he had never even seen them.

But her threat of getting a lawyer? That had cut deep. How had things between them suddenly gone so wrong?

Oh, yeah, he'd gone rogue and not taken into account what Summer would think about his announcement. And now he had to fix things between them once again.

One of Heli-Care's gold-and-blue stretchers rolled by, accompanied by Jo and Summer, and he followed them to the small hospital's only trauma room.

"Mr. Martin is a sixty-three-year-old male who began having chest pain tonight while on a tour of Fort Jefferson," Jo said, which explained the reason why the man had to be flown instead of coming by land with the local emergency services. The Dry Tortugas, where the fort was located, could only be reached by water or air.

As she rattled off the man's vital signs, including an elevated blood pressure, Alex took in the man's color, which was still pink, though his skin did have a sheen of sweat.

"Here's a copy of the EKG," Summer said

as she handed over the paper copy that had been printed off their monitors.

"It looks like an NSTEMI," Alex said as he studied the twelve-lead printout. "Let's get labs and some morphine."

"Mr. Martin, I'm Dr. Leonelli. Can you tell me about the pain you're having?"

"I know you. We watched that interview they did on the TV in our hotel room," the man said.

"Did you now?" Alex said before placing his stethoscope to the man's chest. The man's lungs were clear, but his heart did have an irregular beat. "We need to draw some blood and we are also going to get you something for the pain. If we determine that you need to have a heart catheterization tonight, we'll have to transfer you to Miami so that you can be treated by a cardiac intensivist."

After reassuring the man that his wife would be able to see him as soon as she arrived back from their island tour, Alex went in search of Summer as his team started the workup.

"Hey, boss," Jo said as he entered the room that was set up for the first responders who needed to take a break.

"Hey," Alex said. He watched as Jo pulled out a juice from the fridge and pushed it into Summer's trembling hands.

"What's wrong? Have you eaten?" Alex asked as he bent down to study Summer's color. He took her hand into his and began to take her pulse. "Jo, go get me a glucose monitor."

"No, Jo," Summer said, as color began coming back into her face. "Don't. It's not my glucose. I just bent down to get a drink out of the fridge. I'll be fine in just a moment."

Alex moved into the chair next to her, but he didn't let go of her arm, though her pulse was regular and strong now. "Usually after twenty-four weeks gestation, your blood pressure stabilizes."

"Been reading your obstetric medical books, Doc?" Summer asked before taking a long drink from the juice bottle.

"Maybe," he said. "There's nothing wrong with being prepared."

"Oh, yeah, I forgot. Congratulations," Jo said, her mouth curling up into a smile now that her friend was returning to normal. "Nice job with the announcement, too. I like your style. Most people just go for those little cards they send out in the mail."

"Thanks, it seemed the perfect time," Alex said as Summer removed her arm from his hand while shooting him a look that showed no amusement.

"How many times has this happened?" Alex asked.

"I don't know. I haven't been sitting around counting them," Summer said before finishing off her juice.

Alex looked up at Jo.

"Oh, no. I'm not getting between the two of you." Jo said.

Alex watched as she exited the room. "Look. We're on the same side here. We both want what is best for these babies. Right now, I'm more concerned about what could happen if you have one of these spells while you're at home alone. It's not safe."

"If we were on the same side, maybe we should get our stories straight so that the next time we go on television, we don't end up spilling all our secrets and making announcements without talking about them first."

"What secret? Everyone had to know that these were my babies. We hadn't made a secret that we were dating." His phone rang and he pulled it out to see that it was his brother. He sent the call to voice mail.

"I'm sorry that I didn't talk to you before I made the announcement. I shouldn't have done it before clearing it with you," Alex said, though in truth he wasn't really sorry for anything except for the fact that it had upset Summer. "Can't we put it in the past now? The interview is over, and everyone's attention has probably turned toward some other poor unlucky fools, thank goodness."

"But what if it hasn't?" Summer asked as she sat up in her chair. Leaning toward him, her cheeks now flushed with a rosy glow, her eyes turned serious. "Debbie Duncan seemed very determined to dig up some dirt on the two of us."

"She's just a local television celebrity looking for the latest human-interest story," Alex said, though he had noticed that the woman seemed to have spent more time than necessary with their story. The show had been pitched to Heli-Care's marketing department as good publicity for the company, but instead it had been more about their personal lives.

"About these dizzy spells, I want you to see the doctor as soon as they can get you in and I want you to consider moving in with me," Alex said, and then continued as she started to interrupt him, "What would happen if you passed out and fell? You know well and good that as a nurse you'd recommend that a patient with the same symptoms not be left alone."

"It's perfectly normal for a pregnant woman to get dizzy," Summer insisted, then shrugged her shoulders, "but I'll call in the morning.

And if they think I need to be seen in the office, I'll go in."

"If I promise not to hound you or the doctor, would you consider letting me go with you?" Alex asked, and then waited as she studied him.

"Don't lie. You know that you're going to ask Dr. Wade a million questions. She's already been complaining about nurses making terrible patients," Summer said as she stood. The color had finally returned to her face. "But I'll agree to you coming if you agree to stop insisting that I need to move in with you when she tells you that there's nothing wrong with me."

His phone rang and he was surprised to see the number of the Soura palace on the display.

"Hold on a moment," he said to Summer, then answered the call.

"What? You are screening my calls now?" his brother asked from the other side of the world.

"I'm working. Couldn't you have left a message like a normal person?" He didn't have time to listen to his brother and his insistence that Alex make a decision concerning making a royal announcement about the circumstances of his birth, which now seemed very ironic considering how he'd handled the announcement of his own future children.

"This wasn't something that I could leave until you decided to return my call. It seems our friend from the tabloids has been busier than we thought. There's a picture of a pregnant young woman who he claims is a member of your helicopter crew. He also claims that you, Dr. Alex Leonelli, also known as Alexandro Leonelli, longtime friend of Crown Prince Nicholas, announced on a television show that you are the father. Did you not think this was something you should share with your family?"

Alex swore, getting a surprised look from Summer. While he'd shared his news with his mother, he'd put off notifying his brother and father. He was getting enough pressure from the two of them. Once his father had decided that it would be best to admit to the affair he'd had with Alex's mother, he'd agreed to let Alex make the decision of when to share the information concerning his birth. But that had been before the reality of grandchildren had existed. He wasn't sure how his father would take this news, or how he would respond.

"Sorry, I've been busy. Can you send me the article with the picture?" he asked. "I'll get right back to you."

"Hey, Dr. Leonelli," the unit coordinator said from the break-room doorway, "Dr. Patel is on the phone and Robin said to tell you we have the lab results back on the patient in the trauma room."

"Are you okay to fly if I need to transfer Mr. Martin?" Alex asked, rising from the chair. He wouldn't let this new crisis make him forget what was really important right now.

"I'm fine. I just needed a moment," Summer said as she got up slowly. "What was that phone call about?"

This wasn't the time or place to discuss things, but how could he expect her to trust him if he didn't share this part of himself with her? "It looks like you were right. The journalist from Soura somehow found out about our television interview. My brother wanted me to know that there's been a new article published and they included you and my announcement."

"You hadn't told your father about the babies?"

"Not yet. I was afraid he'd do something crazy like announce that he was going to be a grandfather." The look Summer gave him told him exactly what she thought. Yes, he was living a double standard and, yes, he needed to get his act together.

"I just don't understand why this guy is so

interested in us. You said you've spent time with your brother since you were children, and no one seemed to suspect anything about your relationship then. What has changed? Why would he be so interested in you now, if it wasn't because he suspects that you are the king's son?"

"I don't know, but I'm going to find out. As soon as I get the article I'll forward it to you," Alex said. He wanted to protect her from all the media, but he couldn't do that and leave her in the dark at the same time.

"Thanks. And I'll text you with a time if I get an appointment," she said as they walked back into the emergency room.

As Alex watched her join Jo, who was talking to one of the local EMTs, he realized that for just a moment the two of them had acted like a couple working together instead of two individuals with their own agendas. Maybe this was the beginning of a new path for their relationship.

"So that was interesting," Jo said the moment Summer climbed back into the helicopter after it was determined that the patient's condition was stable, and he would be admitted to the local hospital.

"What?" Summer asked. No matter how

much she might deny it to Alex, she could still feel the residual effects from the earlier drop in her blood pressure. Or maybe it was the anxiety that she felt every time her name was coupled with Alex's in the media. While he was concerned about losing their privacy, she was more worried about the possibility that someone would eventually start wondering about her. It wouldn't take much for someone to dig up her past. A past that would destroy everyone's opinion of her. All she could do was wait for Alex to send her the article that had been published and hope that would be the end of it.

"The way Alex was all concerned about you. It didn't look like a man that didn't care about his girlfriend to me," Jo said. They both worked together to clean and store their monitor cords and supplies, so that they would be ready to respond to the next call.

"Ex-girlfriend. Besides, it's not me he's worried about. It's the babies I'm carrying that concern him." Summer wouldn't tell her friend that he wanted her to move in with him. Jo was too much of a romantic. She'd never believe that it was only an interest in his children that had caused Alex to worry about her being alone.

"There was nothing fatherly about the look

Alex was giving you. I'm not going to tell you what you should do," Jo said, "but if I was you, I wouldn't accept that everything between the two of you is over. Because that man isn't giving up on you."

"You're wrong. If he'd had any real interest in more than just a friendly fling, he wouldn't have left like he did." Summer knew her friend was trying to be helpful. But there was nothing that Jo or Alex could say that could change the past. The only thing her ex was interested in was the two babies that she was carrying. He had made it plain by his actions that he had never meant for them to be more than two friends who became lovers. Whether he had expected them to fall back into that relationship when he'd returned, she didn't know. What she did know was her being pregnant had changed everything. He'd do whatever he had to do to be part of their babies' lives, including marrying her.

And what kind of mother was she that she was jealous of the love Alex felt for her own children? One like her own mother?

Well, that wasn't going to happen. She wouldn't let it. It was time for her to start acting like the responsible mother she wanted to be, and that meant no more wondering about what it would be like to have Alex direct some of the same love and pride he had for their children toward her.

Because no matter what Jo thought, there was no chance of a future for her and Alex. Knowing what she knew about Alex's family now, there never had been. She would never have fitted in. It would take a fairy godmother to convince her that she belonged in his world, and she hadn't seen any of those flying around Key West.

The next afternoon, Summer found herself staring at two little bodies displayed on the ultrasound screen. She counted arms and legs, then hands and feet. They were perfect. Just perfect.

"Their growth is right on target, though baby *A* is a little bigger than baby *B*," the ultrasound tech said to Alex as he studied the screen. The man hadn't said a word since the woman had first applied the probe, with its thick cold gel, to her abdomen.

"Baby *A* is the boy," Summer said, realizing that he hadn't been there for the ultrasound where she had discovered the sex of the twins. Nor had he been there when she had found out that she was carrying twins. He'd missed so much while he'd been off playing doctor to royalty. Not that she had needed him. She'd attended each visit by herself and listened carefully to all the advice of her doctor.

But it would have been nice not to have been alone. Not that it was all Alex's fault. She'd been stubborn, swearing her best friend and then the rest of the crew to secrecy concerning her pregnancy. Because she hadn't wanted to have Alex rush back to her just because she was expecting.

No. She'd wanted him to come back to her because he'd missed her. She'd wanted him to tell her where he'd been and what was so important, more important than her, that he couldn't share it with her. She'd wanted him to reassure her that she was more than just a casual fling that he had left behind.

And what she had gotten instead was a man so entranced by the two babies that they'd made that he had forgotten what it was they used to have together. It was her parents' history repeating itself. She could only hope for her babies' sake that Alex never turned his back on their children, like her father had turned his back on her.

She felt a kick and a thump against her abdomen, and her attention went back to the ultrasound screen.

"Did you see that? That little rascal just

kicked his sister," Alex said, his smile big and infectious.

"Dr. Leonelli, that was your daughter kicking her brother," the ultrasound tech said as she removed the ultrasound probe and gave Summer a towel to clean off the gel. "Dr. Wade will be in soon."

"Really?" Alex said as he turned and stared at Summer's abdomen while she mopped at the sticky gel. "It's amazing, isn't it? The two of them in there already bonding together."

"And a little bit scary," Summer said as the technician left the room. "Can you imagine the trouble that the two of them could get into?"

"Me and my brother certainly got into more than our share, though I can blame most of that on Nicholas, because he knew no matter what, none of the royal staff would go tattling to his father."

Summer found it hard to imagine a life like the two of them had shared. She'd been an only child and spent most of her time alone. "It's nice to know that they'll have each other to play with as they grow up."

"If that ultrasound is any sign of things to come, the two of them will spend as much time fighting as they will playing," Alex said.

The door opened and Dr. Wade came in.

"Well, good morning, you two. It isn't every day I have two local heroes in my office."

"It's nice to see you, Dr. Wade," Alex said as he stood and shook the woman's hand.

"So tell me about these dizzy spells that you've been having," the doctor said to Summer.

As she explained the dizziness and weakness she was experiencing, she kept an eye on Alex. He'd agreed not to interfere today, but the set of his clenched jaw told her it was killing the physician in him to not share his own observations.

"Well, you're right. It does sound like hypotension, as it's mainly when you are getting up or moving too fast," Dr. Wade said. Summer shot Alex a grin. She'd been right. "And I looked over your labs today. Your hemoglobin is on the low side of normal, not surprising, but I think we should increase your iron."

"Is there anything else we can do to decrease these spells?" Alex asked, apparently unable to stay quiet any longer. She had to give him credit, though. He'd lasted a lot longer than she had expected. "She lives alone, and I'm concerned that she's going to get dizzy and fall, and there won't be anyone around to help her."

It was plain to see where this was going.

The man had been insisting ever since he'd found out about the babies that she move in with him.

"Continue fluids and watch for signs of dehydration. You both know how hot it is right now and how fast you can deplete your intake. And just be mindful of the situation. The biggest risk with hypotension in pregnancy is the possibility of falling and hurting not only yourself, but also the pregnancy."

"I told you so," they both said together.

"And you are right, Alex. It would be best if Summer wasn't left alone for now. Maybe a friend could stay with you," the doctor said when Summer protested. "I'm going to order some more tests just to make sure your electrolytes are all good and I want to see you back in two weeks."

The moment the doctor walked out of the room, Summer exploded. "I can't believe you're trying to use a little case of hypotension to make me move in with you."

"I don't know what you are talking about. I just voiced my concerns with your doctor. She's the one who said that you didn't need to be staying alone."

"You've seen my work schedule. I'm only home a few nights a week." She was being manipulated and she didn't like it.

"And that's another thing—I don't think you should be working so much. It's not good for you or the babies," Alex said as he offered her a hand to get off the exam table. She wanted to ignore him, but it wouldn't help her case if she got dizzy and fell in front of him.

"Just take a moment," Alex told her as she stood, his hands going to her sides to support her.

She wondered what he would say if she told him the warm skin of his hand against her waist was doing more to unsteady her than getting up had done.

"I'm just worried you might be overdoing it."

"What do you mean? Dr. Wade just said I was fine." She moved away from him before she did something stupid, like step into his arms. This was why it wasn't a good idea for her to move in with him. Who knew what stupid thing she might be tempted to do?

"She said that there was a risk of you falling if you became too hypotensive. And she said you needed more iron," Alex said as he held the door open for Summer. It had been good news to hear that the lab work looked good, and seeing their babies had been amazing. More than amazing.

He patted his shirt pocket, where he had put a picture he'd been given by the ultrasound technician. He'd have to scan it and email it to his mother. The woman was beside herself with the news that she was going to be a *nonna*. She was already making plans for a visit as soon as the movie she was shooting wrapped up.

"I'm not going to argue with you. I agreed for you to come so that you could see for yourself that I'm fine," Summer said as they made their way out the office.

"I just want you to be careful. And don't give me that look," Alex said when she stopped and stared up at him. "I know you were doing fine before I returned. But I'm back now and I'm going to look out for you. Get used to it."

Alex waited while she let out a deep sigh. Yes, he was being a bit obsessive, but he'd just seen their babies for the first time. Who wouldn't be filled with a sense of responsibility looking at those tiny little arms and legs kicking around in their safe little home? He just wanted to make sure they stayed where they were for as long as was needed.

But that wasn't the only thing. Seeing Summer weak and dizzy scared him. He had to make sure she was safe, too. Because no matter how much she denied it, they needed each

other as much as the two little babies growing in her stomach needed them. Maybe more.
And then there was the article his brother had
sent him.

"We need to talk about the article," Alex
said as they both climbed into the car and
buckled their seat belts. "You were right about
me causing more problems. I'm sorry that I
got you involved in all of this."

"I still don't understand why this reporter
in Soura is so interested in someone who, as
far as the world knows, is just a friend of the
crown prince. He knows something, or thinks
he does."

"My brother's looking into it, but he suspects the man is being backed by someone
who doesn't support the king," Alex said. "Unfortunately, he hasn't been able to locate the
reporter. Which means he could be in Soura or
he could be in Key West. I can't help but worry
that he might show up at your apartment."

"If he does, I'll tell him to go away," Summer said.

How did you explain to someone who hadn't
grown up in the world of the paparazzi how
much of a threat these tabloid reporters could
be? "It's just not that easy. My brother thinks
this guy could be a real threat. He has a reputation for being manipulative and demand-

ing. It would make me feel a lot better if you would come stay with me, at least until this all dies down."

"Why are you so determined for me to move in with you?" Summer asked. Her eyes, so serious, caught his and held. They were such beautiful eyes. So intelligent. So inquisitive. He found them fascinating. They were a true mirror to her soul. A mirror that reflected a yearning for something that he wasn't sure he knew how to give. He reached over and brushed a strand of golden hair away from her face.

Did he tell her the truth? That he had developed this unexplainable need to have her near him? That he didn't understand it all himself, but that he wanted them to figure it out, together? Or would that be the very thing that would make her run from him? She didn't trust him, not anymore. She wouldn't give him another chance to hurt her. He had to earn back her trust before they could possibly have a future together.

He made himself pull away and busied himself starting the car and turning the air conditioner on high.

"It just makes sense, doesn't it? What are your plans when you get ready to bring the babies home from the hospital?"

"What do you mean? They'll come home with me, of course." Summer's chin tilted up. She had a look of determination he was very familiar with. "If you're talking about parental rights, you can talk to my lawyer. I'm not going to agree to one of those split-custody cases, like that movie about the twin girls whose parents split apart."

"*The Parent Trap*? No one with any sense or humanity could do that. I'm talking about where you are going to live. Your apartment is going to be crowded with not only two babies, but two of everything that it takes to care for them." He didn't think right now was the time to tell her that he considered both a mother and a father to be the two things that were necessary to take care of their twins.

"I've already cleared a space where I can fit two bassinets, which will take care of them for the first few months," Summer said. She'd moved across the seat until she was leaning against the car door.

"That's good, but what about your neighbors? Two crying babies are going to be awful loud at night while everyone's trying to sleep. And you're always complaining about the guy next door that likes to play his clarinet at six in the morning. I can't imagine the babies are going to sleep through that."

"Well, what kind of grown man gets up in the morning and starts playing a clarinet? I'll just tell him to stop," Summer said, and then sighed. "I know I need to start looking for somewhere else to live. I just haven't had the time to fight through the rental wars. As soon as something is listed, someone grabs it."

He pulled into her apartment's parking lot and put the car in Park. For a moment, he just stared ahead. It wasn't that her apartment complex wasn't nice, but besides being too small, it lacked security. He needed to find a way for her to agree to this plan for all their sakes. "I have an idea that I need you to consider. I think if you look at it closely, you'll see that it could work for all of us."

He wasn't surprised by the suspicion that filled her eyes. She seemed suspicious of everything he did where their babies were concerned, something that he hoped she'd get over soon. He didn't like that she continued to think of him as the villain in this situation.

No, he wanted to be the brave prince who rescued her by slaying all her dragons, even though he knew she could slay them herself.

"Go ahead. Tell me this plan of yours. Just be aware that I intend on making all my own decisions."

"I understand. I just need you to promise to

hear me out and consider what's best for our children." It was all that he could hope for. He wouldn't force her to do anything she didn't want to do.

"Okay. Spill it," Summer said, her eyes showing him no sign of weakness.

"Things are going to be complicated with two newborn babies to care for. You know I want to be involved, which means I will be spending a lot of time with both you and the babies when you come home from the hospital. It just seems that you staying at my place makes more sense. There's plenty of room at my home. There's a whole wing that could be just for you and the babies. And there's security. I'm sorry I've dragged you into all this, but the truth is that our children are going to need security. And right now, with this tabloid reporter running around trying to find a story, you need to be someplace safe. You would still have your independence to come and go as you please."

He waited for her to explode. He waited for her to throw it in his face once more that she had done everything until now by herself and didn't need him to help her. But she didn't. Instead of taking offence and telling him what he could do with his offer, she just stared at him. Seconds ticked by. Her eyes left his and she looked down at her hands, where they were placed across her belly. He began to fear he had pushed for too much, too soon.

"I know you mean well, and I know right now you want to be a part of these babies' lives, but you need to understand that you can't just commit to take care of them while they're little. If you plan to be a parent, a father to them, it needs to be a lifelong commitment. If you plan to be there for the beginning, you need to be there forever. You can't just go in and out of their lives or, worse, just walk out one day when you get a new job offer or you decide that you want a new family. And don't think that I've lost my mind. Parents abandon their children every day and that's not what I want for my babies. Consider that and I'll consider your offer." She opened the car door, then turned back toward him. "Because I'm more scared of what it would do to my children if you walked away from them after they'd learned to count on you than what danger I'm in from some reporter."

She started to stand, but he reached for her, resting his hand against her back until she turned back to him. "I'm not going anywhere, and I would never leave my children behind. That, I promise you."

He felt the heat of her stare all the way to

his soul. This woman was normally easygoing and lighthearted, but pregnancy had changed her into a momma bear who would not take any chances with her cubs.

Finally, she spoke. "Okay, we'll try it."

He sat there in the parking lot, staring at her apartment long after she had shut the door. There was more here than just a woman who was mad because he hadn't been there for her when she'd found out she was pregnant, though he knew that was part of it. But there was more.

Through all the time he had known Summer, she'd spoken very little about her childhood. He'd not thought that much of it, as he was in a habit of not sharing a lot of his own childhood memories. He hadn't lived the typical lifestyle and always had to be on guard, not sharing anything that would lead back to his father. But now, he knew someone had abandoned Summer, not unlike what he'd done for the five months he'd been gone. Whether it had been her mother or her father, he didn't know. Right now, the only thing that mattered was how he was going to make that hurt go away. And how he was going to make her believe that he would never abandon her or their babies again.

CHAPTER SEVEN

SUMMER WATCHED AS everyone around her worked. Everyone except her. It seemed every time she started to do something, someone appeared at her side to take over. She eyed the man standing at the grill. It was his fault, she was sure.

She'd recently realized that even though the man denied any interest in becoming a recognized member of Soura's royal family, he gave orders and commands like he was sitting on a throne. Like the order that she was to sit and *enjoy* herself while everyone else worked to get this party together.

Yet still, she'd arrived at Alex's with two suitcases, agreeing to give living here with him a try. What had she been thinking?

"I'd be careful with that look. You don't want to set our leader on fire while he's cooking our steaks," Jo said as she came to join her on the oversize lounging chair, where Summer had been basically confined since she'd walked into Alex's home earlier.

"If only that was my superpower," Summer said as she leaned back into the overstuffed cushion.

"He's actually looking hot without your laser-beam eyes toasting him alive," Jo said. "Doesn't his chest look a little more golden since he returned? Maybe he just left us to go work on his tan."

Summer raised her sunglasses and looked back over to the man. She knew Jo was just goading her. Her friend had been trying to get information about where Alex had gone off to ever since he'd returned. But Jo was right. Alex did look good tonight. With his swimsuit trunks—thank goodness, the man had opted not to swim in the buff tonight— and white shirt open against an impressively muscled chest, he looked like just another islander here in the Keys.

Only she knew that was far from the truth, but she wouldn't be sharing that information, or where Alex had disappeared to, with anyone, not even one of her best friends.

She lowered her glasses and leaned farther into the seat. She also wouldn't share how her heart was now pounding and with more than a little interest in the man who had fathered her babies. It was just those hormones again. Those stupid hormones that wouldn't let her forget just how good he'd looked rising from the water in all his sexy bareness.

"You okay? You look flushed. Is it too hot out here?" Jo asked, worry in her voice.

Oh, yes. It was definitely too hot out here while those images of Alex played over and over on some masochistic loop in her brain.

"No, I'm fine," Summer said. Or at least she would be if her pregnancy hormones would give her a break. She did not need to think of Alex that way. Things were complicated enough with a set of twins in their future. Sex with Alex would add a whole new level of complications.

But it was so tempting.

"Moving in with Alex is a good move," Jo said, thankfully changing the subject. "I can think of a lot of places that would be worse living in than here."

Summer didn't have to think of those places. She'd lived in one most of her life. She scanned the yard and pool. Her gaze paused at the outside kitchen, and yep, there was Alex still looking as sexy as he had just moments earlier. She forced her eyes to move on to the back patio and the big sliding glass doors that had been opened so that people could enjoy both the inside and outside at the same time. It was so…perfect. It was everything that the home she'd grown up in hadn't been.

But she wasn't in Texas anymore. She wasn't in the tiny, rusted trailer, or in the small-town high school, where everyone had known that she came from the trailer park. It had been all her mother could afford on her salary from the grocery store after Summer's father had left them. Now she understood she should have been more appreciative, but when she'd been a teenager being bullied by her peers, it didn't matter. She'd just wanted to run away.

Summer knew her children would never be in that situation. She'd worked hard to be independent, with a career that could support her. But was it fair to her children for her to turn down this life for them? Was it fair for Summer to not give her babies a chance to bond with their father? But what then? They wouldn't be able to live in some limbo relationship forever. What happened when he fell for another woman, a woman that could fit in his life better than she ever could? Would he leave their children for that woman?

She looked back over to where he was standing, legs planted securely on the ground, one hand raised in a greeting to one of the local EMTs that had just arrived, while his other hand worked to move the sausages and steaks around on the grill.

A part of her knew that though Alex had let her down by leaving her, he'd never do that to his own children. A part of her was still hurt that he'd left her. That he couldn't have been honest with her and let her into his real life. She knew that part was the little girl in her that had been abandoned by her father, but she still couldn't seem to work through that memory without becoming angry that she'd been stupid enough to repeat her parents' history. And because of that, she couldn't trust her decision-making where her children were concerned.

"You still with me?" Jo said, concern in her voice.

"Sorry, just trying to think things through," Summer said, suddenly very tired. "I guess it's good I'm giving it a try before the babies arrive. It gives us some time to figure out if we can make things work."

"You only have three more months, and you know twins usually come early. But you're right. You have time. If I were you, I'd drag your decision out a bit. Make him work for it," Jo said.

"This is about the babies. Not about me getting some type of revenge. It's not personal." She loved her friends, but right now she wished every one of them would disappear and give her some peace and quiet.

"The look he's been giving you is definitely personal. I know you think things between you were finished after he left, but I don't think he thinks they're finished at all."

"You've read one too many romance books, my friend. Now go join the fun while I close my eyes for a moment. I only got a short nap after I got off this morning. Me and these babies need a minute of shut-eye before this party takes off."

As Jo moved away after making sure the umbrella over the couch was positioned just right, Summer closed her eyes. Her friend was ever the romantic, something that was surprising after the way her marriage had ended, but she was wrong this time. Summer had spent enough time in the last three weeks around Alex to know that he wasn't interested in anything but the babies she was carrying.

She'd told herself over and over that it was okay. Both of their priorities needed to be on the babies right now. But that surely wasn't helping with these determined hormones that didn't seem to understand that their time had passed. There would be no more sexy times between her and Alex, no matter how much they protested.

* * *

Alex watched Summer as he piled the next piece of meat on the already full platter. He knew she'd only gotten off a twenty-four-hour shift a few hours earlier and the dark circles under her cloudy blue eyes were proof that she hadn't had enough rest. How much longer did she intend to push herself? He knew he didn't have the right to order her to decrease the amount of shifts she was working. She was an independent woman who was not going to put up with anyone telling her what to do. Especially not him.

So instead, he'd done the only thing he could do by sending out a message that Summer was not to help with the preparations for the party at all. Now, as she was lying stretched out under an umbrella with her eyes closed, he was glad he had done it, though he knew he'd hear about it later. And he was glad that she'd finally agreed to move in with him. No matter what Summer thought, someone needed to keep an eye on her, and the only person he trusted to do that was himself.

The speakers set around the pool screeched with a sound worse than fingernails against a chalkboard, and the voice of Max, the grumpiest man on the Heli-Care crew, came over loud and clear.

Looking back over at the lounge chair, Alex saw that the noise had awakened Summer, along with probably half his neighborhood. He headed over to adjust the stereo system before Max could damage the ears of everyone attending the party.

"I just thought we should welcome back our boss, who we're all glad has been returned to us—" Max paused while some of the guests clapped "—and also to thank him for this party to celebrate the renewal of Heli-Care's contract here in the Keys."

The crowd, including all the first responders and the scattering of hospital staff that had come to celebrate, broke out in whistles and cheering.

"While I know it was all of our hard work and reputations in our community, we also need to acknowledge both Alex and Summer's heroic efforts that, rumor has it, helped the county board with their decision to continue our contract." Max paused again as the crowd broke out in more cheers.

Alex moved to take the microphone, but the tall Viking of a man, Casey, beat him to it. "Just one more thing, boss. We all wanted to do something for both you and Summer. Not because of the contract, but because you're both part of our family."

Casey turned toward the house, where Alex could now see Jo and other members of both the Key West crew and the Marathon crew bringing out stacks of pink and blue wrapped presents. Somehow all their friends had managed to surprise the two of them with a baby shower.

Turning to Summer, he saw that she was standing. Her eyes were wide with the same surprise. For a moment, he felt self-conscious and a bit uncomfortable that everyone had gone to so much trouble. But then he realized that this was just their way of welcoming what they would consider new members into their family of friends.

He walked over to Summer and took her hand in his. They were in this together. She needed to start getting used to it.

"I didn't know," she said as they approached the tables that were now covered with presents.

"Well, the two of you were acting like you had all day to get ready for these babies," Dylan said as he held Katie's hand.

"Two babies mean two times the stuff," his daughter, Violet, said. "I'm hoping my dad and Katie have twins, too."

"I think it would be best if we take it one at a time," Katie said. "How are you, Alex?"

Alex let go of Summer's hand and gave his old friend a hug. "I'm doing fine. I'm glad the three of you got back in town in time for the party."

When he moved back to Summer, he took her hand again and knew it was just the surprise that kept her from pulling away from him as she had every other time he'd touched her.

As the crowd moved back to the tables where the food had been placed and the stereo speakers vibrated with music, the two of them continued to stare at the presents. It wasn't as if this was the first time Alex had been surprised with a party. His mother had loved to throw him parties as a child, and as everything in Hollywood, she'd always gone over the top.

But this was different. This was for their babies. His and Summer's babies. His coworkers had included him in this celebration, though how Summer felt about that he wasn't sure.

"What am I supposed to do with all of this stuff? They can't really need it all, right?" Summer asked as she picked up one present, then placed it back reverently before picking up another one. It was easy to see that she was overwhelmed by the crew's generosity.

"I've heard that they take a lot of stuff. Let

me show you something," he said as he reluctantly pulled her away.

They walked through the living room, then
turned down a hallway in the opposite direction of his own suite. This wasn't the arrange-
ment he wanted. He'd much prefer to have
both Summer and the babies close to him, but
he knew she wasn't going to accept that pro-
posal. At least not yet.

Opening a door, he led her into the biggest
room on the west wing of the house, where he
had placed her suitcases when she'd arrived.
He'd had a decorator come in the day after
he had asked Summer to consider moving in
with him. While the floors were still the light
natural wood of the rest of his home, a big col-
orful rug now covered a large portion of the
room, where there was a new queen bed and
nightstands. The other side of the room had
been cleared and only a rocker sat in the space.

"I thought that you might want to keep the
babies here in the room with you at first, but
there's the other room across the hall, which
has plenty of room for cribs and all the stuff
the babies will need." At least he hoped it was
big enough. From the mountain of presents
outside, he was afraid he might have to build
an addition onto the house.

"It's so pretty," Summer said as she walked

to the bed and fingered the pale green duvet that covered the bed.

"You can change anything that you don't like," Alex quickly assured her. He'd requested the pale green color as she had once told her it was one of her favorites.

"No, it's perfect," she said as she moved over to the rocker. "You don't play fair, do you?"

"Not when it's something important to me. And you and the babies are important to me."

"You sure it's that and not the fact that you're a spoiled rich kid who is used to getting his way?" she asked.

He knew she was teasing him, but the question did hurt. He'd worked hard not to have the reputation of being that kid who had everything given to him. He couldn't deny, though, that he'd been one of the lucky few who hadn't graduated from medical school with a load of tuition debt. His father had insisted on paying for all of his schooling.

"You know I'm joking," Summer said as she placed her hand against his cheek, her eyes anxious. "I didn't mean it."

His eyes met hers and something from the past passed between them. Something that he hadn't seen in the weeks since he had returned. Was it possible that even though she denied it, she still cared for him? Before she could move back and once more raise the walls she had insisted on putting between them, he lowered his head.

His lips met hers with only the lightest of touches. If she pulled away from him, he'd let her go no matter how much it hurt him. When her eyes closed, and her hand slid down to rest on his chest, he increased the pressure with first his lips and then his tongue until he was sliding it inside her mouth. He captured her moan and released one of his own as his hands swept down her sides and circled her. She leaned into him, her swollen belly pressing against the hard length of him. There was no way to deny his arousal, but neither could she when his hands skimmed over the hardened peaks of her nipples.

"Hey, boss, the girls are outside waiting with some baby-looking cake," Casey called from the living room.

"Please remind me why I put up with that Neanderthal?" he asked as Summer pushed away from him.

"Because despite his size and boorish manners, he's one of the best crew members we've ever had on the team," Summer said, turning her back to him. "It's a beautiful room."

"I'm glad you like it," he said. "We can decide what to do with the other room later," Alex said as he buttoned and tucked in the cotton shirt he'd been wearing earlier.

When she didn't say anything, he followed her out of the room. She might pretend that nothing had happened between them, but Alex knew better. She'd been just as aroused as he'd been. Something had changed between the two of them for those few moments he had held Summer in his arms. She might not trust him yet, but she still wanted him.

He'd accomplished his first goal of having her move in with him. Now he had to win back her trust and show her that they could make things between them work. That kiss had been a sure sign that there was still hope for the two of them. He just hoped that Summer wouldn't let her mistrust of him blind her to that hope.

Summer unwrapped the last present and placed the dainty newborn dress with the stack of other clothes that would need to be washed and hung up in the enormous closet in the room that would be hers and the babies.

"There you are," Alex said as he stuck his head into the doorway. "The last of the crew just left."

"Sorry, I should have helped with the cleanup. The girls helped bring all the presents inside and I just couldn't wait to open them. It kind of makes things more real seeing all the clothes they'll wear and the toys they'll play with," Summer said. Realizing the mess she had made of the room, she stood and bent down to pick up the discarded wrapping paper. "I'll get this cleaned up…"

Her head spun and she felt her body go limp as the blood rushed down to her toes. As her legs began to fold, she gripped the armrest of the rocker and began to lower herself, only to find that she was being swept up into Alex's arms.

"Hold on, let me look at you," he said as he sat down in the chair and held her in his lap. He examined her face and eyes, then took her hand and examined her nail beds.

"I'm okay. Let me up," she said, though she wasn't sure she had the energy to get up if he let her. After the kiss they'd shared earlier, this wasn't a good idea. Even her blood-deprived brain knew that.

"Just wait a minute, and quit wiggling," Alex said, his voice a snarl.

It didn't take but a moment for her to discover why he was being so sharp with her. Her wiggling was causing a problem. A big problem.

"Relax and close your eyes, and it will pass," Alex said.

She was pretty sure he was talking about her bout of dizziness and not his…problem. Still, she couldn't help but enjoy his moment of being uncomfortable. It only seemed right after the last few months she'd spent with morning sickness and now this awful dizziness. It was the first spell she'd had since she'd seen her doctor and she'd falsely hoped they were over.

She laid her head against his shoulder and closed her eyes as the doctor had ordered her to. She was tired. So tired. She just needed to rest for a few moments. It seemed she was always tired. She drifted off to sleep with the feel of Alex's arms tight around her, the feel of his hard body surrounding her. She loved this new protective side of him, though she would never admit that to him. She just wished she knew that it was for her instead of their babies.

When she opened her eyes again, the room was dark, and she was in the bed. An arm, Alex's arm, was lying across her, and his hand was resting against her stomach as if to protect the little ones inside her. Carefully, she lifted his arm and eased from the bed. She needed to find a bathroom. Opening the only door that didn't lead to the hall or the closet, she found a four-piece bathroom. She stared at the large soaker tub longingly. Her apartment only had a shower. The last time she'd soaked in a tub had been the last night she'd spent in the house with Alex. With Alex lying in the bed outside the bathroom door, it was best she didn't remember that night.

She'd already been pregnant then, but she didn't know it. Their life had seemed perfect. Their loving spectacular. And then it had all suddenly ended.

After washing up, she eased open the door and stared at the man sprawled facedown on the bed. He was still wearing the swim shorts he'd worn to the party, but that was all.

She should wake him and send him off to his own room. It was the smart thing to do. The safe thing to do. And she always played it safe.

One of the babies gave her a kick, reminding her that maybe she hadn't played it as safe as she could have. But she didn't care. No matter how much trouble the two little ones got into, she would never have any regrets about them.

She just hoped neither she nor Alex had any regrets for what she was about to do. Because no matter how much she told herself she should run as fast as possible for a woman six months pregnant with twins, she couldn't do it. He was just too tempting. And after the kiss they'd shared, she knew that part of their old life, the attraction and desire, was still there.

She climbed back into the bed, then rolled over to where she could see Alex's face. Oh, there were other things she hoped to see—she had every intention of opening up that dam she'd built around those pesky hormones of hers—but right now she'd just enjoy watching him sleep.

He was such a handsome man, so strong and courageous. He'd never considered his own life when he'd jumped into the ocean to save the young boy, Scottie. He'd given up his own life here in Florida to go help his brother when he was injured, even though he had never been recognized by his family.

His eyes fluttered and he turned over onto his back, displaying his flat abdomen. A line of dark hair ran down his chest and her hand followed it, skimming across his chest, until the soft hair disappeared below the swim trunks. She'd touched him this way many times while he'd slept, patiently waiting for him to wake and take her into his arms. Tonight she was impatient. Her breasts were heavy and a warm tingling heat was gathering between her legs. He hadn't even touched her, and her body was already aroused. She'd read that a pregnant women's libido could increase. Hers seemed ready to set a record.

Her hand had started its path up his chest again when his own hand covered hers. She'd known he was awake by the way the muscles of his stomach had gone rigid as her fingertips had trailed across them.

"Is there something you want?" he asked, his hand holding hers tight over the spot where his heart was now hammering against it.

"Oh, yes. Most definitely." She licked her lips at the thought of all the things she wanted.

His hand cupped her chin, turning her face until his eyes met hers. "Are you sure?"

Sure that this wasn't a mistake? No. Sure that she wanted this, anyway?

"Yes," she said before her head could tell her what her heart was refusing to admit. Whether this was a mistake or not, she wasn't going to turn back now. They'd always been good in bed together. What would it hurt if she just let herself enjoy the moment?

He let go of her chin and shifted to his side until their bodies were perfectly in line. His eyes searched hers. For what? Misgivings? Yes, she had a truckload of those. Even before he'd left—before she'd learned she was pregnant—she'd begun to worry that what she felt for Alex was more than he wanted. She hadn't let it stop her then and she wasn't going to let it stop her now. She'd take what she wanted with no promises of anything but tonight.

She ran her hand up his chest until she cupped his chin, which was coarse with a day's worth of growth. She was filled with memories of the sweet sting of pleasure as the rough bristles had skimmed over the most sensitive places on her body.

Her core tightened. She wanted to feel that sting again. She wanted to wake in the morning with her body marked pink from his attention. She wanted him to get busy. What was he waiting for? For her to make the first move?

She placed her lips against his, much as he'd done earlier in the evening. His lips opened and he jerked away what little control she thought she'd had. He claimed her mouth, her tongue, her breath. She'd opened a geyser of pent-up sexual frustration that matched her own and she loved it.

He rolled her onto her back as one hand clasped the back of her head, then molded their mouths together while his other hand found one aching nipple. He teased its peak through her shirt, setting loose a jolt of heat that headed straight to her core.

She lost all her control. The control that had protected her from all of the dangerous emotions that she'd kept locked away from him. The joy she'd felt the moment she'd discovered he'd returned. The anger she'd felt when he'd ordered her to marry him for all the wrong reasons. The lust she'd felt every time his skin had brushed against hers.

She wanted to hug him, slap him and make love to him, all at the same time. But most of all she just wanted to feel him inside of her again. To feel, just for a few moments, that connection between them when there was no tomorrow to worry over. There was just that one moment in time when they both came together to give and receive pleasure. To share their bodies and their…love?

She pulled away from him and searched his eyes. Was that love or lust she saw there? Surely, it was only lust. She didn't need love.

Her hands followed the path down his chest, over his stomach, until she felt the hard length of him in her hand. This was all she needed right now. Just the passion. Just the fire.

His mouth found her breast as he removed the rest of her clothes.

And then he was inside her, his body hot against hers. There were no words. No soft caresses. There was only the two of them racing for something that had been forgotten and lost. It was there, just outside her reach, but there. His body thrust against her, over and over. She spread her legs to take more. She wanted more. She wanted everything he could give her.

His hand touched that sweet spot between her legs as his mouth latched on to one overly sensitive nipple. She reached one more time for that final peak, her body straining against his, her core tightening around him. Her scream cut through the silent house as she flew apart as bolts of pleasure shot through her, and Alex joined her with a climax of his own.

They collapsed together into a pile of weak limbs and trembling muscles. Her body sated, her mind free of worries of the future, she let herself drift off to sleep, wrapped inside his arms. Tomorrow, she might call herself a fool, but tonight she would sleep without any regrets.

CHAPTER EIGHT

IT WAS THE smell of lilacs that awakened him. He was fond of the flowers that reminded him of a childhood full of hugs and laughter. But this wasn't the scent of flowers. This was the perfume that his mother had once made famous. Which could only mean one thing.

He opened his eyes to find his mother, dressed as if she was going for lunch in downtown New York, standing above him.

"That better be the mother of my grandchildren," his mother said, staring at the two of them with not one sign of self-consciousness.

"What are you doing here?" he whispered. Either Summer was still sleeping, or she was playing possum.

"I told you I was coming for a visit," his mother said. "Is this a bad time?"

Yes, it was a bad time. The worst of times. After last night, he knew there was some hope of him and Summer building back their relationship together. Having his mother drop in was a variable he didn't know if Summer was prepared for. No one was ever prepared for his mother.

But he couldn't tell his mother that. "No, it's fine. Could you give us a few moments, though?"

"Of course, my bambino, I'll make myself at home in the living room."

Not for the first time in his life, he wondered why he couldn't have been born to normal parents. Normal? He didn't even know what that looked like, but it was something he was hoping to give his own children.

He waited until his mother had shut the door behind her. "You can open your eyes now."

Summer's blue eyes popped open, all traces of sleep gone as she flung back the sheets. "Was that your mother? It was, wasn't it? Melanie Leonelli just caught me in bed with her son."

"Since she knows you are pregnant with my children, I'm sure she suspects we have slept together," Alex said as he wrapped an arm around her before she could sprint from the bed. "Stop for a moment."

"But I have to get out of here. I'm not dressed to meet your mother. I don't want her thinking any worse of me than she already does."

He pulled her back into the bed, then tucked her into his shoulder. Summer had made comments like this before. It was as if deep down there was some type of residual shame someone had instilled in her. He didn't think it was about the pregnancy, but there was definitely something that haunted her.

"Stay still for just a moment. You know the doctor said that you needed to get up slowly. You don't want another spell like you had last night." It was probably unprofessional for him to take advantage of the situation, but he needed a few more minutes alone with her before they had to deal with his mother.

Because he knew his mother. When she showed up things always got interesting.

"Right now, I'm more likely to pass out from embarrassment, rather than my blood pressure dropping," Summer said, though her body was relaxing deliciously against him now. If his mother wasn't here…

"You two need to get in here," his mother said from just outside the door. "There's a picture of you two on the television and Debbie Duncan just announced that she has an update on her story with two local heroes after the commercial break."

Summer stiffened against him, and he let

her go after his mother disappeared back down the hall.

"It's probably nothing. Maybe it's an update on Scottie," Alex said. He'd checked on the boy himself and had shared with Summer that the kid was doing great, and his family had returned home.

"Maybe," Summer said. "But I told you that woman wasn't going to leave us alone. She's like a viper. One whiff of blood and she's determined to finish you off."

"There's nothing she can do to us. The only secret we have to worry about is who my father is, and there's no way she's good enough to dig that out," Alex said.

Summer took a moment to look over to where Alex was dressing as she pulled on her own shorts and top. Maybe Alex's only secret was that his father was a king, and, yes, that was a big one, but there were things in her own life that she didn't want discovered. Her juvenile record might be sealed, but it wouldn't take her record being open for Debbie Duncan to find out Summer's dirty secrets.

And then there was the bigger-than-life movie star that was waiting in the living room. It was only logical that Alex would have told his mother that he and Summer weren't a couple anymore. Finding the two of them in bed together had to be surprising. What must the woman think about Summer? That she was fickle?

What did Summer even think about herself? She'd promised herself that she would keep at least an emotional and physical distance between her and Alex, but the first time her hormones started a riot she'd given in.

And it had been worth every bit of the self-incrimination that she was throwing at herself this morning.

"You two slowpokes need to hurry, the story's coming on now," Alex's mom called from the other room. Not yelled, not screamed. No, the woman's voice just seemed to float into the room.

After hurrying down the hallway into the open living room, Summer stopped when she saw the oversize television screen filled with a picture of not only Alex, but also Prince Nicholas. Both men were looking straight at the camera, their matching brown eyes scowling at the cameraman, their imperious noses lifted in a sign of irritation. To anyone with anything close to twenty-twenty vision, it was easy to tell that these two men were somehow connected by blood.

Alex came up behind her, his body going

rigid when he saw the screen. He bit out a mild curse but then quieted when his mother shot him a glare as she turned up the volume.

"Well, don't we have some fun news for our audience today? It seems that local hero Dr. Alex Leonelli has been living a second life, my friends. Not only has he been working tirelessly in our community, but it seems that he's also been taking care of one of the world's most recognized royal members, Prince Nicholas, the Crown Prince of Soura," Debbie Duncan said, speaking to her adoring audience. It was enough to make Summer sick. This woman was about to ruin someone's life and everyone in the audience couldn't wait.

"As many of you may know if you follow the royal community, Prince Nicholas was injured earlier this year in a skiing accident. Exactly how Dr. Leonelli was brought into the picture, we are not sure. It seems possible that the two of them could have met somewhere, as the doctor's mother, Melanie Leonelli, is one of Hollywood's favorites, but no one seems to know for sure. Stay tuned this week as we hope to have more on this story."

The three of them stared silently at the television set as a commercial began to play, then Alex walked over to his mother and took the remote.

"She's just fishing. If she had more, she would have spilled it," Alex said as he turned his back on the television, which was now showing a commercial advertising a local pest cleaning service.

She couldn't help but wonder if she could hire their services to spray the offices of their local television station, because right now, she'd put Debbie Duncan in the category of their biggest pest.

"I don't know this woman," Alex's mother began, "but I don't like the way she is handling this story. The two of you were heralded as two local heroes just a week ago and now you are being dissected for any bit of publicity the woman can get from you."

Summer wanted to high-five the famous actress on her expert appraisal of the situation, but the regal woman would probably think she was crazy. They were already starting on the wrong foot after she'd been caught in bed with her son. She didn't want the woman to think that she wasn't a suitable mother for her grandchildren. She'd have to do better.

"I warned Alex that Debbie was out for more of a story than just the two of us saving a young boy, especially after she learned that we were expecting twins together," Summer said, then held out her hand. "I'm Summer."

"Of course you are. And I have to say that you are every bit as lovely as Alex said you were. I'm sure the two of you have made the most beautiful of babies." Melanie ignored Summer's hand and instead wrapped her in a tight hug.

Summer stared over the woman's shoulder at Alex, who was busy starting a pot of coffee. He gave her a smile and shrugged his shoulders. "Mom, Summer needs to take a breath. She's breathing for three now."

"Yes, she is. And please, call me Melanie. I can't believe Alex has kept you hidden from me for so long. I don't know what he was thinking. There's so much to do to get ready for these two." The woman placed her hand on Summer's abdomen.

The face that had been plastered on hundreds of billboards glowed with a beauty that hadn't been touched by time. Summer waited for her body to withdraw from Alex's mother's touch, as it usually did when someone other than her closest of friends touched her, but it didn't. Instead, both women laughed when one of the twins kicked against Melanie's hand. Who would have thought that two little babies who hadn't even been born could bring together two women from such different backgrounds?

"Well, I'm going to go put my luggage away and then I'm going to call your father, Alex. He'll know how to handle this. He always does."

Summer watched as Melanie swept out of the room. The woman was so beautiful and kind, but still she was a bit much for this early in the morning. What Summer needed was a cup of coffee.

Alex handed her a glass of juice and she sighed. She really needed coffee.

"I'm sorry my mother interrupted us this morning," Alex said as he moved closer.

"It was probably for the best," Summer said. A flush of heat crept up her face. She'd ignored all her rules last night and now she had to deal with the consequences. Which meant she had to figure out where it was safe for her relationship with Alex to go. She'd seen how unhealthy her mom's pattern of going back and forth with her many boyfriends was, and she didn't want that for her and Alex. Or for her babies, who would be even more confused by their parents' relationship.

"I better go. You need to spend some time with your mother," Summer said. She needed to leave before she let the look in Alex's eyes seduce her back into bed while his mother waited for him.

"Aren't you forgetting something?" he asked, his eyes bright with laughter as if he knew her thoughts.

"What?" she asked. It had to be some residual sex hormones that were making her mind all foggy.

"You live here now. You don't need to go anywhere."

She blinked and fought through the fog. How could she have forgotten that she'd moved in the night before?

"I have to go back to the apartment. To pack. To finish packing, I mean." Once more she was making a fool of herself. Today was just one of those days that she needed to go back in bed and burrow under the covers. "I'm just going to go to my room to get dressed first."

"Can you join us tonight for dinner? There's an Italian restaurant in Old Town that my mother loves to visit when she is here," Alex said. "We need to discuss what we learn from my father today."

"I'm sure your mother would like to spend some time alone with you." And Summer needed some time alone, too.

"If Debbie Duncan has discovered who my father is, the media will go crazy," Alex said, then took a sip of coffee. "We both need to be ready for that."

"But I'm not—" she began.

"You are the mother to my father's grand-children. They'll go after any story they can get concerning the two of us. You need to be prepared. Besides, my mother will be disappointed if you don't come."

Summer knew when she had been expertly maneuvered. If she refused now, Melanie could take offence. "Fine, I'll only be a few hours. I don't have a lot left to go through."

"I know it will make my mother very happy." Alex's mischievous smile told her he was going to be using his mother as an excuse for as long as possible. She could only imagine the ways he had used that smile while growing up.

"I need to make it an early night. I'm working a shift for Dylan tomorrow," she said before leaving the room.

Happy to find Alex on the phone when she returned, she hurried out the door before he could stop her.

After last night and then everything that had happened this morning, she needed some time alone. She kept thinking about Debbie Duncan's announcement that had warned of more to come in *their* story. Alex and his mother had assumed that the woman was talking about something concerning Alex. But what if it wasn't about Alex at all? What if the woman had been talking about something she'd found in Summer's background? What would Alex think about her if he learned about her past? How would he feel about her then? She could only imagine, and it what she imagined wasn't good.

Summer thought she knew how the wealthy lived. Her mother had always loved the glitz and glamour of her soap operas, and as a little girl Summer had been fascinated to find that somewhere out there were people who didn't wear clothes from the thrift stores, or eat left-over beans and franks every other night.

But this restaurant and the way they were treating Melanie and, subsequently, her, was so unlike anything Summer had ever experienced.

She'd settled on wearing the one and only maternity sundress she owned. This was Key West after all. A sundress would be considered formal wear in most of the city. Fortunately, Alex's mother had dressed with comfort in mind also, though the flowing dress Melanie had on would probably cost more than two of Summer's paychecks.

"Christos is looking into Debbie Duncan," Melanie said as soon as the waitress walked away. "He told me about the journalist in Soura that has been asking questions of the staff concerning you and Nicholas, and that you saw him here. Neither one of us like that."

"Are we sure that he isn't the one that been encouraging these questions?" Alex asked. "He's been pushing for me to come forward and acknowledge him."

"I thought he was the one that didn't want to acknowledge you," Summer said, sure that she hadn't misunderstood what Alex had told him about his birth.

"Times have changed. When I first met Christos, we knew that his country would not accept me, an outsider, as their queen consort even if his father hadn't already become involved in looking for his son's wife. Now things are different," Melanie said with not one hint of bitterness.

"And with all the social media and all the journalists looking for the next big story, like our friend Debbie, my father thinks it would be best if we controlled when my existence is released to the public."

"I think you both worry too much. If it comes out that you are Christos's son, so what? His father and wife have both left this world. His country loves him and will stand behind him no matter if he had hidden three or four children," Melanie said.

"He hasn't, has he?" Alex asked.

"No, my bambino. Your father was always true to his wife, until her death."

Summer wondered how the woman could be so sure. Was it possible that Alex's mother and father had more than just a past relationship? It did seem that the two of them had remained close. Maybe that was a sign that there was a glimmer of hope for Summer and Alex to remain friends.

The waitress delivered their first course, a creamy Italian soup covered with Parmesan cheese.

"Excuse me," a woman asked as she approached them. "I just wanted to tell you, Miss Leonelli, how much I enjoy your work."

Summer watched the rest of the night as Alex's mother graciously signed autographs and talked to other patrons.

"Was this what you had expected when you decided to go into acting?" Summer asked as the last fan left their table.

"It was a long time ago, but I don't think I really considered it much. I had been in theater since I was very young. After college, it just made sense that I would go to California.

I worked hard, became the star I had always dreamed of being and raised my son. The fans and paparazzi are just a small part of my life."

Later, as she prepared for bed, Summer thought about the difference in how Melanie accepted her fame and the attention that she dealt with daily, while Alex was fighting against having to accept his father's world and the attention that would come along with it. From the outside, it was easy for Summer to see that while the paparazzi were part of the job for her, Alex had never wanted that fame.

She thought about how quiet Alex had been during their meal. It would be easy to blame it on the stress of worrying about what the Miami morning-show host would broadcast next, but he'd shown no signs of being unhappy on the way to the restaurant. It had only been when his mother had become the center of attention, pulling Summer and Alex into the other restaurant patrons' focus with her, that he had become quiet and withdrawn from their conversations. It was plain for her to see that Alex preferred to be left in the background, which was the real reason he was still fighting to keep his connections to the royal house of Soura buried. It wasn't that he didn't want to have a normal relationship with his father and brother. He just didn't want the attention that would come with it.

She didn't think either his father or mother understood their son in that way. He wanted to be the person in the background that helped the man who was experiencing an MI or the child that had a fever.

He'd chosen a job a world apart from his mother's. He'd chosen to help people through medicine. There was no fanfare. No applause. There was just the satisfaction that you had made a difference in someone's life.

He wanted to live his life without having to worry about phones recording him as he tried to revive a young man on the beach. And that was what he wanted for their children.

Unable to sleep, Summer headed to the kitchen for a glass of milk. Seeing the light from the television was on, she hesitated. She didn't think running into Alex right now was a good idea, since every time she looked at her bed, her face heated with memories of the night before. She was glad to see that it was his mother instead.

Dressed in a long sleep shirt and boxer shorts, Melanie looked almost normal, making Summer feel comfortable dressed in her maternity pajamas that were covered with pink flamingos.

"Sorry, I don't mean to disturb you," Summer said. There had been a time when Alex's home had felt like her own, but now she felt out of place, like a visitor that had overstayed her welcome.

"I'm still stuck on another time zone. I just thought I would watch some television before I headed to bed. Come sit beside me for a minute and tell me what's bothering you."

"Why do you think something is bothering me?" Summer asked as she opened the fridge. After pouring herself a glass of milk, she joined Alex's mom on the couch.

"Why do you think there's something wrong?"

"As an actress, I study people's expressions. I can see the worry on your face. Is it that Debbie woman?"

This was an opportunity for her to learn more about Alex. All she had to do was stop thinking of Melanie as a movie star and instead think of her as a mother.

"No, not really. I mean she's part of it. She does seem to be focusing on us and I can't figure out why."

"She's a journalist, so she smells a story, though she might not know what it is yet," Melanie said.

"Maybe, but her I understand. It's her job

to look for stories, to find something about us that no one else knows. I still don't like it, but I know it's not personal." Summer pulled her legs up on the couch and looked at the woman next to her. The lights were down low and shadows played off the older woman's face.

It was now or never. "Alex has explained why he grew up unable to tell anyone about his father. I know you didn't have a choice, not then, but it must have been hard for you to raise him on your own."

"I never felt that I was on my own, not with Christos calling every day checking on the two of us. I always knew he would be there if I needed him. Are you worried that Alex won't be there to help? Because I can tell you he will be. My son is a very responsible man."

"Oh, I know Alex is responsible," she said, then took a sip of milk. Summer just didn't want to be another responsibility to the man.

"But why did you let his father even be involved with Alex if he couldn't be a real father to him?"

"I never blamed Christos. He was as much a victim of the situation as Alex. I knew that if he could, he would have done things differently, but his father was old-fashioned, and he never would have accepted Alex. In his way,

Christos protected Alex from a life where he would have been shunned."

"But it had to have confused Alex when he was young." Summer suspected that it still confused the man that Alex had become. He was so determined to live quietly out of the spotlight, but he'd been quick to drop everything and rush to his father's side when his brother had been injured.

Melanie pulled her feet onto the couch, then turned toward her. For a moment, Summer thought she might have pushed too hard. She didn't want Melanie to think she was judging her. If anything, Summer was amazed at how well-adjusted Alex was, considering it had been a childhood spent dodging cameras and playing the part of a fatherless boy.

"I'm sure he was at times, though I tried to make his life as normal as possible," Melanie said, a bittersweet smile following her words.

"I didn't mean to imply you did anything wrong," Summer responded, than drank a little more milk.

"I know, dear," Melanie said before moving closer to Summer and covering her hand. "If you could have seen the look on his face when I'd tell him he was going to visit his father, you'd understand. He loves his father, and his father loves him. The fact that they've had to hide that has been hard on them both, but it would have been harder if Christos hadn't been there at all."

"But he seems so determined to keep his relationship with his father a secret," Summer said, wondering, not for the first time, if Alex was wrong to hide himself from the world. Maybe if he admitted to the everyone who he really was, he could finally have the open relationship any child would want to have with their parent. "It's almost like he's ashamed of who he is, which doesn't make sense."

"You forget, Alex grew up in a Hollywood spotlight. From the time he could crawl, he was the subject of the media's curiosity about the identity of his father. By the time he was a teenager, he couldn't leave the house without a bodyguard. Living in my world is hard for any kid. Alex spent his school years trying to blend in with the other kids as much as possible, but that's difficult when your picture is plastered on the tabloids at the grocery store. It seemed everyone was either jealous of him, or they wanted to be his friend just to enjoy some of the attention he was getting."

Summer had been bullied enough in school to understand Alex wanting to blend into the background. It was a lonely place, but it was better than the pain.

She tried to cover a yawn as she stood. The milk had done its job and she knew she needed to call it a night. She had a long shift ahead of her the next day. It seemed the further along she got in her pregnancy, the longer the shifts were.

"Thank you for answering my questions. I don't mean to be nosy. I just…" How could she explain her feelings for her son to this woman, when she didn't understand them herself?

"It's okay. You're carrying his babies. It's only natural that you would want to know more about his life before you met him."

"His life has been so different from mine." And Summer was beginning to understand that her children's lives would vastly different from what her life as a child had been.

But wasn't that what she had always wanted? Only now, it didn't seem enough that they would never have to miss a meal or do without the simple things a child needed. She had always wanted to give her kids the one thing she'd lost when her father had left—a family.

"I don't know what happened between the two of you, but I can tell you Alex has shared information about his family that he has never shared with anyone before. That tells me that he trusts you, and it takes a lot for Alex to trust. He's been burned too many times by people who said they were his friend, but only cared what his friendship could do for them."

"I won't do that to him. I won't use him." No matter how tempting it might be to accept the security he was offering her.

"I know that. So does Alex. He trusts you. Now you just need to decide if you are ready to trust him," Melanie said. Rising from the couch, the woman moved to Summer and pressed a motherly kiss against her cheek. Summer's hand went to her cheek and her eyes filled with tears as Melanie left the room. This woman who barely knew her had shown her more affection than her own mother had in years. But was it an act? Or, like Alex, was she willing to do whatever was needed to be a part of Summer's babies' lives?

Was this what it had been like for Alex when he was growing up? Never knowing who cared for him and who wanted to use him? If so, she could only feel sorry for the little boy. No one deserved to feel the pain of wanting someone to care for you while being afraid it wasn't you they really wanted.

CHAPTER NINE

ALEX TRIED TO read the latest corporate email for the third time. When his boss had informed him they had been able to retain the county contract, he hadn't bothered to mention that they had promised the county a price cut. A cut that was being passed on to their local budget. Now it was up to him to find where he could make those cuts.

With the size of the population, the Keys were unable to maintain a large hospital, so the service of a medevac helicopter was a necessity. In the five years he had been been there, they had added a second helicopter located in Marathon and their service stayed busy throughout the year, between transfers from the local hospital to Miami and transport from the beach or accident scenes. It didn't make any sense that they were being asked to cut back to cover costs.

Standing, he stretched out his back. He was

tired and cranky after a sleepless night and an early shift in the emergency room. Unfortunately, he already knew he wouldn't be sleeping any better tonight than he had the night before, because the woman he wanted to be sharing his bed would be sleeping here at headquarters tonight.

After their night together, he'd hoped she would join him in his room, but she'd continued to remain on her side of the house, and he couldn't understand why. The desire between them had been just as strong as it had been before he'd left. Didn't that prove there was still something that connected the two of them? He just needed to find a way to get her back into his bed. Then he'd work on keeping her there.

The sound of the helicopter landing on the helipad beside their headquarters filled the building and he relaxed. It always made him feel good when his crew returned safely from a call. Having Summer out on the calls this far into her pregnancy was especially stressful.

He met them in the kitchen. From the look of the crew, it hadn't been an easy call. All three of them clearly needed some rest. Hopefully, the remainder of their shift would be quiet. "Everything go okay?"

"Winds were a little rough," Roy, their pilot,

said before moving past him with a bottle of his favorite soda product.

"The transport went fine, but our patient wasn't looking so good when we left. Septic shock from an infected knee. We had maxed out her IV pressure support before we landed. I'm not sure she's going to make it," Summer said.

Was that worry that was shadowing her eyes, or was she just tired? This was the second extra twenty-four-hour shift she'd picked up this week. It needed to stop.

"She should have come in earlier. Her husband said he tried to get her to cancel their trip after she had knee surgery, but she was determined that they were going to spend their anniversary in the Keys. I just hope it isn't their last anniversary," Max said, then moved past him.

"Is it possible that he's even grumpier than usual today?" Alex asked as he watched the man head into his sleep room.

"He might be. He's mainly been speaking in grunts and growls," Summer said.

As she took a chair at the kitchen table, he took the one opposite. He reached down and lifted her foot into his lap, then began to untie the laces of her boots. When she didn't pull her foot away from him, he moved to the next one. The moan she released when he began to massage her feet sent a spark of desire through his blood. The swelling he found when he got to her ankles doused it.

"You have to stop working these extra shifts," he said as he kneaded the pads of her feet. She closed her eyes and stretched back. When she didn't answer, he thought she might have fallen asleep.

"Are you speaking as my boss or as these babies' daddy?" she asked as she rubbed her hand over her stomach, as if trying to soothe them.

"What if I'm speaking as a friend?" Alex asked. And what if he was speaking as her lover? Would that allow him the right to be concerned for her?

"I need to work, Alex. I'm saving so that I can take a few months off after the babies are born," Summer said.

"You know that isn't necessary. You know I can take care of you." He couldn't understand why she was being so stubborn.

"Do you know me at all?" she asked. "I don't want or need anyone to take care of me. I left home the day I turned eighteen and I've paid my own way since then."

"If we were married… Wait a moment," Alex said as Summer began to pull her feet from his hands. "I just need you to listen to me for a moment before you explode. I just want you to consider what would have happened if things had been different. What if I had told you about my family before I had left? Or what if there'd never been a reason for me to leave at all? What if things between us were like they were before I left? We had something special. You know we did. What if you had discovered that you were pregnant then? Would you have married me?"

"But you did leave me. That's reality. Things changed. We can't just turn back time. We're not the same people we were then." There was no anger in Summer's voice as she said the words. And that scared him. She'd given up on them.

"It sure didn't feel like that when you were in my arms. How can there be nothing between us, yet we can still make love that way? You can deny it all you want, but I felt it. You still want me, and I still want you. Nothing there has changed." If she thought he was going to give up on them, she was very wrong. He'd glimpsed what he had lost, and he wasn't giving it up again.

"That was just sex. Just like all the times before was just sex," Summer said.

"You know that isn't true," Alex said, letting go of her feet as she pulled away from him and stood.

"You weren't honest with me," Summer said. She was looking down at him now, arms locked across her chest. She was as closed off from him as she had been the day she'd marched across his lawn and declared that they were having a baby. "Why, Alex? If I'd meant something to you, why did you leave without telling me? Why didn't you trust me with your secrets?"

As painful as it might be for her, he needed to break through to her if he had any hope of them getting back to where they had been before he'd left. Because he hadn't been just trying to persuade her when he'd said they had something special. It had been special. They'd been special together. And he wanted what they'd had back.

"I know you're angry at me for leaving. But that's not the entire problem, is it? Someone left you. They left you and they didn't come back. Who, Summer? Who hurt you?" Alex said, getting up and stepping toward her, then brushing her hair from her face.

A crash sounded down the hall and the two of them sprang apart. For a moment, he had forgotten where they were.

"What was that?" Roy asked as Alex passed him as he came out of his sleep room.

"It came from Max's room," Summer said as she joined Alex at the other man's door.

"You okay, Max?" Alex asked as he knocked on the door lightly. He didn't want to startle him. Maybe he'd simply knocked something off his bedside table.

When a deep moan came in answer to his question, Alex tried the doorknob. It was locked.

"Here," Roy said, handing him a privacy key that was kept above the doorframe.

After the door was unlocked, Alex pushed into the room, only then realizing that Max was lying on the floor, blocking the door.

"Get the pack from the helicopter," Alex said to Roy as he leaned down to Max and began an assessment. A lamp was lying broken by the side of the bed and the nightstand by the door had been turned over. It looked like Max had been trying to get to the door for help before he had fallen. Max's skin was clammy and his hand was clutching his left arm. Alex didn't have to ask if he was feeling pain. It was etched into every wrinkle on his face.

This had either come on fast, or his friend had been ignoring his body's cry for help. Lifting his arm, Alex checked Max's pulse. It was fast but strong. His respirations were fast and labored. The man needed an EKG as soon as possible.

"When did the pain start?" Summer asked as she rushed to his other side.

"Watch the glass," Alex warned her.

"It wasn't bad," Max said. "I thought…indigestion."

"You know this isn't indigestion," Summer said as she began her own assessment. "Are we flying local or are we headed to Miami?"

She didn't ask who would replace her partner on the flight. She knew Alex would be going with her.

Roy returned and handed Alex the EKG monitor. The pilot had been working as a medevac pilot long enough to know what they were looking at. Max was having a myocardial infarction. They just needed the EKG reading to confirm.

While Summer applied the electro patches for the monitor, Alex pulled a stethoscope from the go bag and listened to Max's heart and lungs. While his breathing was fast, Max's lungs were clear.

"Any allergies, Max?" Summer asked when she pulled a small container of medication from the bag.

"Just penicillin," Max stated, taking the chewable baby aspirin Summer handed him. "Can you call Stacey? She'll be worried if I'm late coming home in the morning."

Alex looked at the reading on the heart monitor. Max wouldn't be coming home in the morning, and they all knew it.

"You're having a STEMI. We could take you to the local emergency room, but that would just be a waste of time. You need to be in Miami, where they have an interventional cardiologist and a cath lab available," Alex said.

There was only a nod of his head from Max, but it was enough. "Roy, contact Dispatch and let them know we're flying one of our own to the city."

"I'll get the stretcher," Summer said, following Roy out to the copter.

"I can walk," Max said, though he didn't attempt to get up.

Alex would let the man have his pride. It was hard for someone used to being the caretaker to find themselves on the other side of the stretcher.

"We'll get you on some oxygen and morphine as soon as we get you loaded."

Max grunted an acceptance. Just more proof that the man was hurting.

Alex saw that Summer had her boots back on when she brought the flight stretcher. As they loaded Max, Alex noticed the difficulty she was having lifting the stretcher up. Whether the stubborn woman wanted to admit it or not, her hours of flying were about to end.

But that was a problem that would have to wait. Right now, he had to keep his concentration on Max.

They were in the air in record time. Alex contacted the Miami emergency room and sent the EKG strip to confirm what was wrong with Max. A cardiologist and their cath-lab team would be waiting for them as soon as they landed.

"What can I do?" Alex asked as he ended the call.

Summer might have had trouble with getting up and down with the stretcher, but she was running the flight single-handedly, as if she flew solo every flight. She'd already started an IV and hung fluids.

"His heart rate is in the one-thirties and his blood pressure is one hundred and eighty-eight over a hundred and two, both possibly elevated due to pain. I've given him five mg's of morphine. I'm going to repeat it in five minutes."

"Oxygen?" he asked. Max's normal ruddy-colored cheeks had turned ashen.

"He's on five liters with an oxygen saturation of ninety-five percent," Summer said.

"How's the pain, Max?" Alex asked.

The man opened his eyes and gave his boss a thumbs-up before closing them again.

"I'm giving him another five mg's of morphine now," Summer said as she pushed the IV medication.

It was so frustrating that they couldn't do more for him. If he was in an emergency room, he could be ordering tests and speaking with the cardiologist himself instead of depending on some doctor he had never met to pass on all the correct information.

"ETA, three minutes," Roy said into their earphones.

"We're almost there, Max. These guys are going to fix you up as good as new," Summer said as she patted Max's hand.

As the skids touched down, Alex could see the hospital crew waiting for them. In seconds, Max was unloaded and headed to the cath lab, where the team was waiting for him.

"What are we going to do?" Roy asked.

"I can fly back with Roy and call in someone to take the rest of the shift with me," Summer volunteered, though Alex could see that she didn't want to leave her coworker.

"Roy, if you can call Dispatch, I'll call the

Marathon crew and let them know they're covering all the Keys until I can get a second crew together," Alex said. "Summer, if you can call Jo and get her to go to Max's and get Stacey, I'll start calling the rest of the crew."

With everyone assigned a duty, Alex and Summer headed into the emergency room while Roy lifted off to head back to headquarters.

"Did you find a crew?" Summer asked before taking a seat in the waiting room outside the cath lab, where they'd been told they could wait.

"Dylan and Casey are headed in now," Alex said. "You?"

"Jo's headed to Max's to get Stacey, but they're still hours out," Summer said, taking a seat on a waiting-room couch that didn't look like it had been bought for comfort. She'd been tired when she and Max had returned from their last flight together. With both her feet and her back aching, she couldn't have flown another call tonight.

Alex was right. She couldn't keep continuing working like this. A lot of women continued to fly while pregnant, but she'd never known one to do it carrying twins. She'd saved up her vacation time and she had her savings to help cover her time off. If she started picking up shifts in the emergency room, she would be able to cover most of her leave. Because no matter how much Alex insisted, she wasn't going to let him support her. Somehow, she would make it work.

Her eyes slipped closed, and her mind drifted off to a place where there were no worries about bills or work. She felt someone lift her legs onto the couch and undo her shoes. A blanket covered her, and she snuggled into it. Alex. He wasn't really a bad guy. She thought he might have a hero complex, though. Always wanting to take care of her.

It was as if he truly wanted to be that Prince Charming who saved poor Cinderella. She'd spent her own life taking care of others with no one ever taking care of her. What must it feel like to be rescued like that? Not that she would ever know. After all, she would never be princess material.

It was the sound of her name that brought her out of her dreams. And Alex's name. Someone, a woman, was talking about her and Alex. Was it his mother? No. Alex's mother didn't even know Max. There was no reason she would be here. It had to be Jo or Stacey. They were coming to the hospital. But if was them, she'd slept a lot longer than she should have. She needed to get up and check on Max. She just needed another moment to rest her eyes.

"When interviewed, Prince Nicholas, the Crown Prince of Soura, refused to comment," a woman said, her voice carrying across the room from the television.

Summer's eyes flashed open as she expected to see Debbie Duncan's morning show on, but this woman wasn't the blond host who'd been giving updates about Summer and Alex for the last week. This woman was older, her natural brown hair lacquered in a perfect dome around her face. Her plain black glasses gave her a look of authority.

No, this wasn't the Miami morning-show host. This was someone a lot more dangerous.

"Sorry, I left you. I had hoped you'd still be asleep," Alex said as he rushed back into the room. "I stepped out with the cardiologist to see Max. He's in recovery."

Summer ignored him as she searched the cushions for the remote. It had to be there. Where had it gone?

"What's wrong?" Alex said.

He was staring at her like she was a crazy woman. Maybe she was. Had she dreamed the whole thing?

Her hand touched something hard and plastic under the last cushion on the couch. Bingo.

"They were talking about us on the television," she said as she used the remote to back up the television until a picture of Prince Nicholas came on the screen. She went back farther until there was a picture of both her and Alex together—a picture she had never seen before.

"Someone was following us the night we went out with my mother," Alex said. He walked closer to the television, where a picture of Alex and Summer at the restaurant with his mother was frozen on the screen.

Summer hit Play and they listened to the news anchor relate the story of their rescue of the young boy, Scottie, and the information that had come from Debbie Duncan's morning show about the two of them expecting twins.

When the picture of Nicholas came on, Alex took the remote from her and turned up the volume. "Further investigation has led to some speculation that there is some connection between the royal family of the Mediterranean country of Soura and this doctor. Something that the small country's population has now taken an interest in. When questioned by a Soura journalist, Crown Prince Nicholas refused to make any comments, something seen as unusual for this outspoken member of the royal family."

The woman ended the segment and went on to what had to be more newsworthy than a story about a doctor and pregnant nurse.

"I need to make some phone calls," Alex said.

Summer watched him pull out his phone and begin to scroll through his contacts. "Max is okay?"

"Sorry, yes. Two stents to the blocked vessels and the prognosis is good. They'll take him to a room on the cardiac floor as soon as he's more awake and you can see him there," Alex said as he punched a number on his phone.

Expecting that he was calling either his father or his mother, she was surprised to hear him talking to a lawyer. Who had a lawyer's personal number? Who had the nerve to call a lawyer this early in the morning? Someone who had a Hollywood star as his mother and the king of a country as a father, it seemed. She and Alex came from such different worlds.

And that fact would be even clearer if Summer's own past came to light. What if someone got in touch with her mother? Their contact with each other had been minimal since Summer had left home. Her mother had never understood why Summer had needed to leave and had made it plain that she'd expected her daughter to stay to help with the bills. Summer sent her mother a check each month to help. It was all she could do for the woman who had raised her.

"I just spoke to Jo," Alex said as he walked over to where Summer was staring out the window, as the sun began to rise. "They should be here in another hour. She's going to stay with Stacey until Max's brother gets into town.

"As soon as they get here, we can take a car to the airport. My mother is having her pilot meet us there."

She couldn't help but be impressed that the man only had to ask to have a private jet at his beck and call.

"Look at you, acting all princely," she teased. Not that there was anything funny about the situation that both of them were in. "How did the two of us go from local heroes to international celebrities?"

"This is my fault. I should have refused to do the interview with Debbie no matter how much pressure I was under from the guys in marketing." Alex started to run his hands through his hair.

Before she could stop herself, her hands began to comb through the dark brown strands, smoothing the ends back down. "It's not your fault. Maybe the interview wasn't the smartest thing we did, but you saw that look in her eyes. Debbie was going to get a story from us no matter if we did the interview on not."

Alex shook his head—whether in agreement or denial, she wasn't sure. He had to be as surprised as she was that the local morning-show reporter was helping to break open a story that his parents had managed to keep hidden for over thirty years.

A half hour later, Jo and Stacey had been deposited in Max's room, so Summer and Alex headed to a small private airport. After arriving and embarking, the pilot requested they buckle their seat belts just as Alex was finishing his last call. Since it had been in a language she didn't understand, only the look on his face told her the discussion had not gone well.

"The story on the Miami news is correct. That journalist who followed me here has run several articles concerning my mother and father's friendship in college, and how I have spent time in the palace since I was young. While my brother and father have refused any comment at this time, there has been a meeting arranged with the prime minister."

"Which means?" Summer asked.

"Which means that my father is probably considering all his options. He could just let this blow over, or he could decide to send out a royal announcement concerning my birth."

"Would that be like those little baby-announcement cards Jo was talking about?" Summer asked, not surprised when Alex didn't get the humor in the situation.

"You're not taking this seriously," Alex said. "If he announces I'm his illegitimate son, the sky will rain down reporters on us. They'll be everywhere."

Alex waited as an attendant brought in two trays and placed one on each of the tables in front of their seats. "Is there anything else I can get you?" he asked.

Summer lifted the tray and found a full breakfast of eggs and bacon, along with potatoes and fruit. One of the phone calls Alex had made must have been to place an order for their meals.

"This looks amazing, thank you," she said to the man.

"Is this what your life was like before you moved to Key West?" She couldn't imagine it. Alex had always been so self-dependent.

"Sometimes, when I traveled with my mother, but most of the time I was at home," Alex said.

"Where you had a private cook and a nanny, I'm sure," she said. When Alex just shrugged his shoulders, she let it go. How could she ask someone who lived like this to understand the way she had lived? He'd never appreciate the things that living in poverty had driven her to do when she was young. "Maybe it won't be that bad. They're a world away. Your father could be right and it's just time to let everything out in the open. Maybe you're just fighting the inevitable."

"If it means keeping my privacy and protecting you and my children, I'll fight it until the day I die."

And by the fury in Alex's eyes, she knew he intended to do just that. She could only hope he wouldn't regret it.

CHAPTER TEN

SUMMER PLACED THE last of her clothes in the huge walk-in closet as she listened to Jo's update on Max. The man was back to his grumpy self, which they both considered a good sign.

She'd taken a long nap only to find that Alex was still tied up in phone calls when she had awakened. It seemed his mother had suggested a reputable personal publicist, who could handle any stories that broke concerning her and Alex.

"I need to tell Alex everything," she said, interrupting Jo as she was critiquing the care their coworker was getting in the big-city hospital.

"And that's a problem?" Jo asked.

"You know it is," Summer said. It was so hard not to tell her friend the truth about Alex. How had he lived with this secret for so long? Not that she didn't understand secrets. Her own secrets were not something she wanted to share. She didn't want to see that look of disappointment in his face. And what about his mother? If Summer's past came out, she'd never be able to face Melanie again.

"You were young, Summer. It's not as big a deal as you think it is," Jo said.

It would definitely be a big deal if it was splattered all over the internet and TV screens that the mother of Prince Alexandro Leonelli's twins had once been a teenage shoplifter.

"Just get it over with. Does this mean that you've accepted his offer and are moving in with him for good?" Jo asked. "Because personally, I think it would be good for both of you. It will take some of the financial pressure off you. You can't keep working the way you are for much longer. I bet you can't even see your toes anymore, can you?"

Summer looked down over a rounded belly that seemed to have grown overnight.

"Yes, I can see my toes," she said as she wiggled her toes in a thick rug that covered the closet floor, happy that she could still see the tip of both of her big toes. "And, yes, I'm staying with Alex for now. But I'll be staying on my side of the house," Summer said before her friend could get any ideas.

"For now," Jo said, following with a laugh. "Want to make a bet on how long it takes for

one of you to find your way to the other's side
of the house?"

"No, I do not," Summer said. She didn't
want to think about their sleeping arrangements. So far, she had managed to keep herself away from Alex's bed, though she'd been
tempted. But the two of them had enough complications as it was. Alex had already turned
their one night of sex into a sign that they had
a future together, something she would deny
no matter how her heart was arguing with her
brain.

Besides, his mother was staying on his side
of the house. There was no way she would take
a chance at getting caught sneaking into the
woman's son's room.

"Seriously, Summer, Alex isn't going to
judge you for something that you did when
you were a kid. He probably has his own secrets. We all have something we're not proud
of."

Summer knew some of Jo's own secrets.
Her friend was determined to feel responsible
for her ex-husband's actions. Not the abuse—
Jo knew that wasn't her fault. It was the fact
that she'd waited too long before she had left
that still haunted Jo.

And she couldn't tell her friend that there
were a lot of people that might be judging her

really soon if the story broke on Alex, and Summer got dragged into it.

Once more, she was reminded of the burden Alex had lived with all of his life. It made it a little easier to understand why he had been so reluctant to share things about his life with her. Like why he'd leave the country without sharing where he was going. He'd grown up hiding from the attention his mother lived with. All he'd ever known was that he needed to keep anything that had to do with his father a secret.

Maybe Melanie was right. The fact that Alex had shared his secret with her now had to have been difficult for him. It had been a true sign that he did trust her now.

She was still thinking about what Melanie said later that afternoon, when Alex appeared at her bedroom door.

"Would you like something to eat? My mother made up some sandwiches for us before she left," Alex said.

"She's gone?" Summer asked, not sure if that was a good thing or not. It had been nice to have a buffer between her and Alex in the evenings.

"You were sleeping and she didn't want to disturb you. It was decided that her presence here could add to the attention we receive.

She'll be back soon, though. She's so excited about the babies. She'll take on all of the paparazzi if they get in her way when they're born."

Summer had no doubt the woman was up for the challenge. She'd managed to raise a son out of the limelight. She had to be very talented in avoiding the reporters.

"My father is just as happy, though I know he won't be able to come to the States anytime soon."

She didn't even want to think about what having a king for a grandfather meant for her children. Having her children keep the kind of secret Alex had lived with wasn't something that she could imagine.

"Sandwich?" Alex asked again. "I've been stuck on the phone all day. We can eat outside by the pool."

As they carried the food outside, Summer could see the lines and shadows under his eyes from his lack of sleep in the last twenty-four hours. She hated to be the person to add to his worries.

"Did it go well with the publicist?" she asked.

"As well as it could. My mother assures me that the woman has been trusted with secrets much bigger than ours," Alex said.

She had to tell him now. "I was arrested when I was seventeen for shoplifting," she said, the words pouring out of her mouth without a filter to lessen the awfulness of the truth.

She waited for Alex to react. She waited to see the shock, the disappointment she expected. But none of it came. After laying down his sandwich, he turned his eyes to her. But it wasn't disgust or disappointment she saw. Was it sympathy? She didn't need his sympathy. She'd had enough of that growing up. Sympathy from the teachers when she didn't have half the supplies from the school each year. Sympathy from the food-service workers who snuck in extra servings of food that weren't covered by the free-lunch program. Sympathy from the few friends that weren't too embarrassed to be seen with her in her hand-me-down clothes purchased at the thrift store.

"It was a long time ago, but I thought you should know. You should probably tell the publicist, too." Unable to sit there a moment longer, she stood and left the table. She wondered if his mother would suggest he count the silverware now.

Alex waited a moment before following her inside. She needed a moment to deal with whatever this whole media mess had dragged up in her past. Whatever had happened in her childhood was causing her a lot of pain. They'd never finished the conversation they'd had before Max had collapsed and he knew that they were tied together.

"I'm sorry," Summer said when he stepped in the room. She was sitting on a rug, where various baby clothes had been separated into stacks. She looked so young, so innocent.

"I don't understand why you are apologizing. You have nothing to be sorry about," he said as he took a seat beside her. He picked up a tiny aqua-and-orange football jersey. He laid it down, then picked up a pink dress with ruffles around the edges. It was hard to comprehend that in just a number of weeks there would be a baby boy and a baby girl wearing these. They were so tiny.

"How did I get here?" Summer asked.

Knowing it wasn't meant as a question for him, he didn't respond. He suspected that she had taken a path much different than the one he'd taken that had brought him to the Florida Keys.

"It was only through scholarships and student loans that I managed to even finish nursing school. These babies will be in college by the time I get those loans paid off," she said, rubbing her abdomen.

She'd never mentioned the loans before. Probably because she knew he'd offer to pay them for her.

"And this..." She spread her arms and looked around the room. "I never imagined anything like this for me."

"What did you imagine?" he asked. Knowing where Summer came from and where she had planned to go might answer a lot of the unanswered questions he had about who had hurt her.

"Freedom. Escape. A life far away from my hometown. Independence," Summer said. She leaned back and stretched out on the carpet. Staring up at the ceiling, she smiled. "What do you call all this fancy woodwork on the ceiling?"

Stretching out beside her, he studied the wooden framed panels that covered the ceiling.

"It's a coffered ceiling," he said. "It's just an architecture feature. If you don't like it, we can have it removed."

Her laugh wasn't one of humor. "See. You don't like something you just have it removed. I looked up at the same water stain over my bed for my whole childhood. My whole bedroom would fit inside of your closet. Twice. I can't relate to your life. It's too foreign. Just like my life growing up would be foreign to you."

"It didn't seem that we were that different before I went away, did it?" he asked. "Am I so different now?"

She turned her head toward him; her lips were barely a breath from his. Her hair smelled of sunshine and honeysuckle. Had he moved closer? Or had she?

"No, you didn't. It seems I had done a good job of putting that time of my life in the past. But the past is always there. Your past. Your parents' past. My past. My parents' past. It's always there," she said.

"Tell me about it. The part of your past that's bothering you now," he said. Leaning over her, he brushed his hand across her cheek. "I've shared my secrets. Trust me with yours."

"There's certainly no king hidden in my ancestry. That, I'm sure. My parents grew up in the same little town in Texas as I did. The paper mill was the biggest employer there. Something you'd know if you ever drove through the town. There's no mistaking the smell of a paper mill." She turned her face back to the ceiling. "It probably wasn't as bad as I imagine it. I think I just saw the worst of the place. Not that there's really any good place to grow up poor. To say I grew up on the wrong side of the railroad tracks would not be wrong, except we were almost on top of the tracks, since they ran right beside our trailer."

"I'm sorry your childhood was so hard," Alex said.

"It wasn't always bad. For the first few years I think I was happy. We had food and clothes. I don't remember thinking I was any different than my friends then."

"What changed? Who left you, Summer?" he asked.

"My daddy left when I was around five. Or maybe six. I should know that, shouldn't I? But it doesn't really matter. He married my mother when she got pregnant. The marriage lasted a few years. More than a lot of marriages in those circumstances. End of story. Not much different than a lot of people's story."

So that was why she'd gotten mad when he'd suggested they marry. At least that was part of it. There was sure to be something deeper than her parents' failed marriage.

"So things were hard for you and your mom when your father left," Alex said.

"Hard? We lived on my mother's grocery-store paychecks. I helped when I got old enough to work. I babysat, cleaned houses. I even worked at one of those automatic car washes, where you get paid by the day. But it was never enough. So when things were a little short at the end of the month, I learned how to pick up a few things at the store without getting caught."

"Do you think I'm going to judge you because you got caught shoplifting at the grocery store when you were hungry?" he asked. Her body was so tense. He wanted to take her in his arms. He wanted to feel her relax against his body. He wanted her to trust him to take care of her.

"No. I don't think anyone would condemn a kid for stealing some food when they were hungry. I'm pretty sure the people at the market knew what I was doing."

"But you can't forgive yourself?" he asked.

"If I'd stopped there. Sure. That's not what I'm worried about the media getting a hold of. It's the four-hundred-dollar dress I stole for senior prom. How do you think it's going to look if it comes out that the mother of King Christos's grandchildren went to jail for stealing a stupid dress?"

"Was it at least a pretty dress?" Alex asked.

"What?" she asked as she turned toward him. "What difference does that make?"

"I just think our publicist should know what she's dealing with. It would be a lot better if she knew that you at least had good taste."

"You're joking, right?" she asked.

"It's okay, Summer. Do you really think my father, after raising my brother, Nicholas, is going to be shocked because a teenage girl wanted a pretty dress for her senior prom?"

"But the media..." she said.

He pulled her against him, then rested his forehead against hers. He reached between the two of them and rubbed his hand in circles over her abdomen. "Let me take care of the media. You have enough to take care of with these two."

She leaned her head on his shoulder and for that moment things were all right with Alex's world. Tomorrow the paparazzi might be chasing the two of them down. Tonight, they were together.

"You really don't care, do you?" she asked, her voice breathy and sweet.

"Do you believe that this one thing in your past defines you? You're an excellent nurse, a great friend and you are going to be a great mother to our babies. That's who you are, who you've become. It might not be what you imagined for your life, but you can be proud of the person you are."

His hand brushed back her hair and he kissed her forehead, then continued a path down to her temple and her cheek. He pressed a kiss behind her ear to that secret spot that brought a gasp from her lips. Her body arched into his. His hand went to another hidden spot behind her knee before running it up her bare legs until it met the fabric of her shorts.

"Don't stop," she said as she began to unbutton his shirt.

"Never," he said, before continuing his dual paths, his lips trailing down to her lips while his hand traveled up to the juncture between her legs.

He kept his kisses gentle, teasing her lips until she opened hers in a sweet smile.

"You're tired, let me…" Her voice broke on a gasp as his hand dipped under her shorts.

"I'm fine. Better than fine," he said as his fingers touched her soft folds. She was so wet. For him. She wanted him and there was nothing he wanted more than her.

She moved against his fingers and his own body strained against the bonds of his clothing. He wanted to pleasure her, to fill her. To make love to her, taste her and excite her until she couldn't imagine a life without him touching her. Adrenaline shot through him with that thought and his heart sped up to a dangerous rate. Holding himself back might kill him, but he wouldn't rush this for her.

He rolled her onto her back while she still

fought against the buttons of his shirt. He ripped it from her hands, scattering buttons across the room as he flung it to the side.

"Now you?" he asked, knowing this woman didn't like demands. The cotton T-shirt landed beside his shirt. Her bra followed. "Your shorts?"

She arched her back to push down her shorts and he ran one finger between her folds before plunging it into her. She gasped and her legs tightened around his hand as his finger continued to pump inside her. He could enter her now, end this torture for both of them, but she refused to take anything from him. He could give her this first.

His mouth kissed the top of each of her pretty breasts. Her skin smelled of the same honeysuckle as her hair.

Her breath caught as his lips continued down until his mouth took one tight nipple into his mouth. He sucked hard and her core clenched his finger. She was so tight and needy.

He ran his thumb between her slick folds as his finger pumped inside her until the sound of her labored panting filled the room. He took another deep suck as her body arched up against his hand.

"Mine," he growled before his lips took

hers, swallowing her gasp with a kiss that held none of the gentleness he'd shown her before. His tongue tangled with hers as her core throbbed against his hand, her legs tightening around his hand as she rode out her climax.

His body was on fire with the need to take her. Such a primal need. Such a humbling weakness. His life's breath seemed to depend on this one moment.

His shorts disappeared. Had he removed them or had she? When her hand clenched the length of him in her tight fist, that mystery was solved. She guided him into her, her breath coming as fast as his.

"More," she demanded.

He answered her demand with one thrust straight to the deepest part of her. She answered him back, taking him deeper, faster, with each stroke. There was nothing left in their world as this frenzied need to mate engulfed them.

Her body exploded around him as a new orgasm gripped her, taking him with her as his own orgasm tore through him.

A weakness like he had never known filled Alex's limbs. He rolled to his back, taking Summer with him. Her hair tickled the inside of his arm, where her head rested on his shoulder.

The axis of his world had been changed forever. He had turned into some primal male who had just marked his female as his own. Did she know? Had she felt that desperate need that had driven him? This woman was his now. He'd fight for her and their children with every breath of their body. He could never leave her.

And he would prove it to her if it took every moment of the rest of his lifetime.

CHAPTER ELEVEN

"YOU KNOW HOW much I hate these things," Summer said. Being part of the crew that got stuck having to take part in the show-and-tell day at the local elementary school wasn't her idea of a fun outing, no matter how much her boss tried to sell it to them. Over a hundred kids running back and forth between a helicopter, an ambulance and a police car had disaster written all over it.

She was going to use the pregnancy card, but Alex was already making some noise about grounding her. After she'd weighed in that morning, Alex had made their new pilot, Sam, confirm that she was not over the weight limit with the fuel they were carrying.

He'd been joking, mostly. And she really couldn't complain. For the last week, the man had been totally undemanding.

Except in her bed, which he had somehow taken over. Her hormones had never been so happy. And if she was honest, neither had she. She was playing a dangerous game with her emotions, but she was willing to risk it.

He'd even listened to her thoughts about when she would need to stop flying altogether. She'd made it to thirty weeks. She knew her days of flying were numbered, but he'd finally agreed, as her boss, to allow her to fly as long as her physician said it was safe and she could still do her job. He'd argued that as the father of her babies he deserved an extra vote in the matter. He'd lost that argument. She'd agreed that she would continue to stay with him for the rest of the pregnancy and at least the first few weeks after the babies were born. She refused to tell him that her happy hormones had helped him with the vote on that one.

"I would love to go with you, but I've got an afternoon shift at the hospital, and I still have to deal with implementing some of Corporate's new policy changes," Alex said.

"Maybe we'll get lucky and there'll be a pileup on the highway," Jo said, her perky but sadistic smile making Summer wonder if she was serious.

"It's not that bad. It's only for an hour," Alex said as his phone rang. The sharp look he gave her said it was one of two people, his father or his publicist. A call from either of them could contain bad news.

"Let's go," Summer said to Jo. "We're not going to talk him out of it."

"I think we should ask for hazard pay," Jo said.

Summer pulled the door to Alex's office closed behind them. Her friend looked back at the door and her eyes narrowed.

"When are you going to tell me what's going on? Every time I turn around Alex is on some hush-hush phone call. I know it has something to do with all those rumors hitting the internet. The ones about him being tied up with some royal family. That's where he went, isn't it?"

Summer wanted to tell her friend everything. She wanted to spill her guts. She'd even discussed it with Alex. Their crew could be trusted. They'd been nothing but protective when some of them had been contacted by the press. No one had commented when they'd been asked about their boss's disappearance.

But no matter how much she thought it would be better to just tell all of Alex's secrets so that they could move on, it wasn't her place. He'd trusted her and she wouldn't let him down. For now, they would just wait out the rumors.

"You know how much he's got on him right now. Debbie Duncan and all the things she's saying will die down soon," Summer said, not believing her own words. If she'd learned anything since she and Alex had been dragged into this mess, it was that the more someone learned about them, the more they wanted. No matter what Alex said, the local reporters smelled blood and they weren't going to stop hounding them until they got the last drop.

The hour flew by as one child followed another in an organized line, as much as you could organize a field full of kids, up to the helicopter. Each one took their turn sitting in the passenger seat while Sam talked about the basic parts of the helicopter and Jo explained the medical equipment they used. Summer had set up an impromptu safety-education post using their stretcher as a table, along with some of the supplies donated by the ambulance crew stationed beside them. She needed to have Alex talk to the corporate office about providing some give-away items for the kids.

"How about a chair?" one of the teachers said. It was a nice offer, considering the woman looked like she was dead on her feet herself.

"I'm Kathy. That's my class by the police

car. I just wanted to tell you how much we appreciate you taking your time with the kids."

Summer winced. She shouldn't have complained about having to take time out for these kids. This poor woman managed to handle them every day. And one day it would be Summer's own kids running and playing on this field. Maybe Kathy would even be their teacher.

"We appreciate you, too. I have to admit I would be more comfortable scraping up some poor accident victim off the road and loading them into the copter for a ride to the nearest emergency room." The look the woman gave Summer told her she'd been a little too honest. Not everyone understood the humor of first responders.

"You're that woman on the beach from the video, aren't you? The one that helped save that kid from drowning?"

It seemed she would be known as "that woman on the beach" forever now. "If you are talking about the video where the real hot guy risked his life to save a young boy, yes, I am."

The teacher laughed as her cheeks turned rosy. "I'm being rude. I'm sorry."

"It's okay. It's been an interesting experience going viral." Summer could only hope it would be her last. But with her children having a Hollywood star for a grandmother, she was doubtful. Was it too much to ask to spend a quiet life in the islands? She was beginning to understand why Alex was fighting so hard to keep his identity a secret. How would she ever know if someone wanted a play date with her kids or if they just wanted to say they knew the grandchildren of Melanie Leonelli?

Another group of kids descended on her and she went through some safety rules that she hoped would keep these kids out of her helicopter, then she handed out some cartoon bandages.

Even with sitting in the chair, her back was aching by the time the last group of children headed back to their class.

"Next year we're sending Max and Casey," Jo said as she climbed back into her seat in the helicopter.

Summer had no idea what next year looked like for her. She'd have two babies to consider then. Finding childcare for twenty-four-hour coverage for one child would be hard. She had to find someone willing to do it for two babies.

She didn't want to admit it, but staying with Alex would at least take some pressure off of her finances. And if things continued as they were, maybe the two of them could work together on the childcare problem. Alex had said he wanted to be a hands-on dad. She just hoped he realized how many hands he was going to need with twins.

The voice of a dispatcher came over their headphones. Summer and Jo groaned in unison.

Their pilot laughed as she changed their course. "Three-vehicle MVA on the Highway One bridge. It looks like your wish was just running a little behind schedule, Jo."

By the time they had returned to headquarters, the pain in Summer's back was throbbing. She carefully sat down into the first recliner she came to. "I can't go another step."

"I thought they'd never get that guy out of the car. How he managed to escape with only a broken femur and a few crushed ribs, I don't know," Jo said as she passed by on her way to the kitchen.

"Can you bring me a water?" Summer asked. She knew she was behind on her fluid intake. Constantly chugging on a water bottle wasn't an option when you were ten thousand feet in the air.

Closing her eyes, she laid her hands across her belly and took deep breaths. Something wasn't right. Instead of the pain in her back subsiding, as it usually did when she put her feet up, it was getting worse.

Her eyes opened when she felt the cold of a bottle pressed into her hands.

"Are you okay?" Jo asked. Her friend's eyes went into nurse mode.

But it wasn't what Summer saw in her friend's eyes that alarmed her. It was the picture of a woman on the television screen across from her.

"I need to turn up the sound," Summer said as she pushed the bottle back into Jo's hands and started to stand.

"I'll get it. You sit down," Jo said, grabbing the remote and turning up the volume on the local news channel.

"Summer's mother states that she has been estranged from her daughter since Summer left home at eighteen and has not been back. Her mother blames the fact that Summer turned her back on her family on the fact that Summer had a problem with always wanting more than what she had, claiming that her daughter had been caught shoplifting and had spent time in jail."

"Yeah, I wanted more. I wanted to have food in the cabinets when I was hungry and clothes that weren't worn out and stained when I got them. What kid doesn't want more when they're made fun of because of the way they dress or where they live?" All of a sudden, her body became cold and clammy. She was glad she was sitting because she knew her weak legs wouldn't have been able to support her. "Jo, call Alex. I need Alex."

"It's okay. No one's going to listen to those reporters. We all have things we wished we hadn't done as kids. And you had every right to want more than what you had as a kid. No kid should ever go hungry."

"I don't care what they say. Not now. Right now, all I need is for you to call Alex and tell him we're on the way to the hospital. I'm pretty sure my water just broke."

Jo's face turned white as her eyes locked on the puddle of water between Summer's legs. They were both experts in the smell of bodily fluids.

"Maybe it's just a leak," Jo said, always the optimist. Not even a plumber would call the size of the puddle that Summer was sitting in a leak.

"Contractions?" Jo asked as she laid her hand across Summer's abdomen.

"Maybe. I've been having some back pain all day. I didn't think anything of it. I'm only thirty weeks. I'm not supposed to have contractions yet," Summer said. There was panic in her voice, and she fought to control it. She needed to stay calm for her babies.

Insisting that flying would cut down on the drive time to the hospital, Jo went to find Sam while she called Dispatch, leaving Summer alone with her fears. She should have known something was wrong when the back pain didn't go away. She should have listened to her body more. She should have listened when Alex told her to cut back on working, even though she knew she needed the money to provide for the babies.

What if something happened to the babies because she had been too proud to let Alex help her? How would she be able to live with the knowledge that she'd let her pride come before them?

She looked up at the television screen, which had shown a picture of her mother just seconds before. Her own mother had spilled all of Summer's secrets.

No matter what happened, Summer would take care of these babies. She would protect them with her life. She would not lose them.

CHAPTER TWELVE

ALEX WAS FURIOUS the moment his publicist called to tell him about Summer's mother being interviewed. How could a woman say things like that about her daughter? It made him wonder if Summer's home life as a child had been even worse than she had admitted.

"Dr. Leonelli, there's a call coming in on the radio for you. It's from the flight crew," said Anna, the charge nurse.

"Go ahead," Alex said into the radio, his voice sharp and clipped. He reminded himself that no matter what was going on in his personal life, he needed to remain professional. It wasn't unusual for him to receive calls from the crew for instructions when they had any medical-care questions. It was part of his job as medical chief of the crew.

"Alex, this is Jo. We're bringing in a patient for OB triage. Thirty weeks gestation, premature rupture of membranes."

Jo knew the process for caring for the pregnant woman in flight. They had specific procedures in place, including transferring any preterm pregnancy to a Miami hospital unless the delivery seemed imminent. They were seldom involved until they received a call from the hospital for transport because most preterm patients arrived by car or ambulance. Why was this woman even being flown?

An uneasy feeling settled in his stomach. Summer was primary nurse today. Why was Jo calling instead of her? "Jo, let me talk to Summer."

"Now is not a good time," Jo said.

"When?" he asked. PROM at thirty weeks was not common and Summer hadn't had any signs of preterm labor. At least none she'd shared with him.

"Just a few minutes ago," Jo said. "I've only palpated one contraction and it was mild. She says she feels the babies moving. All she wants is for you to call Dr. Wade for her. We have an ETA of three minutes."

Alex's fingers were already speeding through his contacts on his phone.

"Give me her vitals. How's her blood pressure?" He knew that her problem wasn't her hypotension. This was something entirely different. Something unexpected. Thirty-week babies had a good survival rate. But there could be complications. There always could be complications with twins.

"She's okay, Alex, I promise," Jo said.

He was waiting at the emergency-room doors as Jo and Sam rushed through with the stretcher carrying Summer. "I told them I could walk, but they refused to let me. It's like I'm talking to two strangers."

Just the sound of her voice calmed his fears. His heartbeat settled into a steady rhythm and his breathing became easier. She was okay for now. They would tackle the rest after the obstetrician examined her, though he had already begun to make inquiries about which hospitals had the best NICU unit in the Miami area.

"I told her to shut up and enjoy the ride," Jo said, as she pushed the stretcher through the emergency room.

"The labor and delivery nurses are expecting you. I'll be up there as soon as my relief gets here. She agreed to come in early for me so it won't be very long." Alex couldn't leave the emergency room uncovered though he wanted nothing more than to be with Summer.

"Text me if you need me," he called after them as they headed down the hall that led to the elevator to the L&D unit. He stood and watched them until they disappeared into the elevator. He didn't want to be one of those overbearing fathers. He'd give them fifteen minutes to get Summer to her room and the monitors applied before he called and started hounding the nurses.

As he went back to his desk to finish up discharge orders on a patient, he remembered the call he'd received from the publicist. The last thing Summer needed was to hear about her mother's interview on the television while she was lying in a hospital bed. Who knew what that would do to her? He needed to protect her. He pulled out his phone and began to type.

Jo, try to keep Summer from watching any television.

Seconds later her reply came over his phone.

Too late, boss. She's already seen it.

When?

Right before her water broke. She's handling it. She's stronger than you think.

Stronger? His publicist had told him that her mother had made hard, cold comments that were sure to damage Summer's reputation.

He didn't care about Summer's reputation, or his own. All he cared about was her and the babies. Was watching her mother's interview what had caused this? Had the stress been too much, sending her into labor?

This would never have happened if it wasn't for him and the rumors coming from Soura. He'd tried to protect her, but it seemed he had only made things worse.

The first beat of Baby A's heart started a trickle of Summer's tears. When the beat of Baby B's heartbeat joined in, the trickle became a waterfall. She would never in her life hear such a beautiful sound. The sound of both heartbeats, with each beating its own rhythm while still blending together into a beautiful ballad. She'd managed to keep a calm facade, never letting Alex or Jo see just how scared she was, but she couldn't hold it in any longer.

"Dr. Wade called and is only five minutes out. I did inform her that you were still leaking fluid and that it had tested positive for ROM ruptured membranes.Besides monitoring, she's ordered an ultrasound for dating the babies' gestation age and estimating weight, and also for measuring amniotic fluid. Do you have any questions for me?" the nurse asked.

"I don't think so. Not now." She was sure

she would have a hundred questions before this was over with.

Summer had never felt so much out of her element. Labor and delivery was one of the few areas she hadn't worked as a nurse. Give her a severed limb or a cardiac emergency and she was fine. Give her a patient in labor and the most she knew was how to catch the baby, resuscitate it if necessary and keep the mother from bleeding out. All the testing and monitoring that she knew she was in for now was just foreign. What she did know was that it was too early for these two to be born.

"You just need to stay in there a little bit longer, guys," she whispered to her little ones. She placed her hands against her belly and laughed when one of them kicked against her hand. They were strong and active babies. Everything was going to be okay.

"Would you like me to turn the television on for you?" the nurse asked.

"No," Summer said. Her voice seemed to bounce around the oversize room, startling both her and the nurse. Even the babies responded with a flurry of movement. She couldn't stand the thought of these nurses hearing the interview that her mother had given. At least not while she was a patient here. After what her mother had said to the press, everyone would think that she was some gold digger.

"Sorry, but no. I don't want it on." She might not even want to turn on a television again after seeing how the truth could be twisted so easily. She'd done the crime and she'd paid the price. Shaming her now only had one purpose and that was to raise ratings. Why would someone like Debbie Duncan or any of the other people who called themselves reporters ever be interested in little old her? Oh, yeah. Because she was carrying his babies. She suddenly remembered that she had forgotten to warn Alex. "Can my friends come in, though?"

"Sure, I'll get them. And Dr. Leonelli called to say he'd be here in just a few minutes."

Once the nurse was gone, Summer tried to relax in the bed. Her back still ached and occasionally she felt a tightening spread over her abdomen that might be a contraction. Fortunately, they were very far apart.

She watched the labor monitor for a few minutes, remembering enough from nursing school to understand what all the squiggly lines stood for. She assumed since no one was rushing in the door that none of the lines showed anything ominous.

But soon she was bored and began taking

in the rest of the room. It was a pretty room, decorated with a floral wallpaper of bright pinks and greens against a white background. The whole place had a happy vibe, though she wasn't sure what was up with the fluffy couches that were so big that they could seat up to seven or eight people. What was it people did here that they needed that size of an audience?

Still, the place was so different than the emergency room that was just one floor down that it was fascinating. They could have been different realms. Happiness was not something you found in the emergency room. If you were happy you didn't go to the ER. Except maybe Max, if he was going around feeling happy someone might want to rush him into the hospital. They'd heard from his wife that he was being a horrible patient. It wasn't a surprise.

Her stomach tightened and she took in a deep breath the way she'd coached pregnant patients to do when they'd had to fly out of Key West.

A coach? She didn't have a coach. She hadn't even taken any classes for labor. She and Dr. Wade had planned a C-section because of the twin factor. What if they couldn't stop her labor? Would they do a C-section today?

They didn't have even have car seats ready. The cribs that Alex had helped her pick out were still in their boxes. They weren't ready for any of this.

Before she could panic, a new nurse came into the room carrying a tray of supplies and a large bag of fluid, along with another, smaller bag. Summer recognized the med as soon as she read the label. They were going to start her on IV magnesium sulfate in order to stop her labor? So she was in labor and they were going to try to stop it? What if they couldn't? It was much too soon for these babies to come into the world. She'd assumed that she'd just be on bed rest for a few weeks until the babies were old enough to deliver.

She should know better. She was a nurse. She looked at the clock on the wall. Where was Alex? She needed him to be here.

And when had she gotten dependent on Alex? Since he'd come back and inserted himself in every part of her life? No, in their babies' lives. Not hers. Just the fact that she wanted him right by her side was scary, though. They were getting too involved. She was getting too dependent on him. Because she was too in love with him? So in love that she was forgetting all the reasons why she couldn't trust him? Forgetting that he might someday disappear like he had before? Like her father had disappeared?

She tried not to flinch when the nurse stuck the large bore IV needle in her arm at the same time that another contraction had started. Were they getting closer together? Looking at the monitor, she tried to measure out the minutes.

The door opened and the man she had been thinking about too much entered the room, followed by her obstetrician. She wasn't sure which one she was the most glad to see. And that was a big problem. One that she would have to deal with later because the serious look in her doctor's eyes said she wasn't going to like what she had to say.

"How are you feeling?" the doctor asked as she looked over to where the nurse was busy taping up Summer's IV.

"I've had a couple contractions, but they weren't bad. More like cramps," Summer said, trying to stay positive, no matter that the nurse was programming an IV medication that would make her feel flushed and lethargic. She remembered that from nursing school, too. Not that it would make any difference.

"I'll do whatever it is to keep these babies inside of me," she blurted out as her nerves finally got the best of her. She really didn't like to be on this side of the bed. She wanted to be the one making the decisions. Not waiting for others to make them for her.

"I know you will. That's what we need to talk about. The ultrasound tech should be here soon, and I need to perform a pelvic exam. Then we'll talk about our next move. We definitely want to get some steroids on board for the babies, so the nurses will give you your first injection here."

"You mean the next move as in to transfer me to another hospital?" Summer asked, though she knew the answer. She'd always known she couldn't deliver preterm babies here.

"I'm afraid so and probably soon. I just want to confirm that you're not dilated and are safe enough to fly first. Your contractions are not regular, so that's a good sign, and the mag will slow them down if not stop them altogether."

From then on things seemed to move faster than she could keep up with, partly because the magnesium drip had her light-headed and nauseated. She felt like she'd partied too hard the night before, not a feeling she was fond of.

And Alex sat beside her bed the whole time. He'd held her hand while Dr. Wade had examined her. He'd held her hair when she'd been sick from the medicine. And when Dr. Wade had declared her safe to fly, he'd been on the phone making arrangements for her transport while giving Katie the access code to his gate and house so that she could pack bags for the two of them.

She remembered about needing to tell Alex about her mother, but then realized his publicist had probably already contacted him. It was what he was paying the woman for. He wouldn't have mentioned it to her because he didn't want to upset her. Right now, with the worry for the babies, nothing her mother could have said would have bothered her. But he didn't know that.

He was so determined to take care of her and the babies—babies he'd only known about for a month, but whom she knew he already loved as much as she did. How had that happened so fast? The same way she had begun to realize she was in love with him? Had always been in love with him?

"You don't have to fly over with me. For that matter, I don't see why I'm not going by ground. Dr. Wade says I'm barely dilated, and the babies are doing great. The mag is doing its job. I'm stable." It was the second time Summer had gone over this with him, but he wasn't hearing her.

So, less than two hours from when her water

had broken, Summer found herself once more on the wrong side of the helicopter. She wasn't a fan. It was a lot more fun sitting up in the seat watching monitors and landscape instead of being stuck staring up at the ceiling on an aircraft. Still, it was better than lying helpless in a bed while people scurried all around her. Fortunately for all of them, the hum of the rotors put her right to sleep.

CHAPTER THIRTEEN

ALEX KNEW IT wasn't a good idea the moment they turned on the TV to the television-and-film award show. He was trying to keep Summer insulated from all the Hollywood gossip that they had suddenly become a part of. While he'd been approached multiple times now by reporters wanting information about him and his connection to Soura, Summer had been protected inside the hospital, where no type of press was allowed. Knowing that had made it a lot easier for him to work the last week, though he returned to Miami every other day.

It was the nights when he couldn't return to the hospital that were hard to endure. He'd found he preferred sleeping in a chair at Summer's side, the sound of the babies' heartbeats in the background, to returning home to a house that was quiet and empty. How had his life changed so much?

"I feel like we should have popcorn or something," Summer said, sitting up with her legs crossed in the bed. Now that the mag had been discontinued, her face once more had a healthy glow and she had returned to her happy self. It had been hard to watch her suffer through the side effects of the medicine.

"I can see if the nurses have some, though I think this is more a champagne type of event," Alex said.

"If I had popcorn I'd throw it at you right now," Summer said as she acted out throwing imaginary popcorn at him.

"I can see I'm going to have to take you to the Oscars next year," he said, brushing the pretend popcorn from his shoulder.

"What? You can do that?" she asked. "You're joking, right?"

"No, I'm not joking. I'm sure my mother could get us in if you want to go."

She seemed to think about it a moment before she shook her head, her happy mood now gone. "No, I don't think that's something I should do."

Alex could understand her reluctance to put herself out there after all the publicity they had recently gotten. Instead of the media's interest dying down, it had increased when news of Summer's preterm labor had broken. It seemed the public had taken an unusual interest in the two of them. His brother had called earlier that day with the news that the television stations in Soura were showing clips of Alex that had been recorded over the years. With so much focus on their lives, his brother had encouraged him to speak with their father. Alex sometimes felt like he was on a train heading straight into a dead-end tunnel with no way to stop the collision ahead of him.

"It's your mom, there," Summer squealed, and the rustle of sudden baby movement came over the monitors. She rubbed at her belly. "Sorry, guys."

There was more movement over the monitor and then the steady sound of two heartbeats returned.

"She sent me a picture of the dress. Isn't it amazing? Look, the host is going to speak to her. Turn the sound up," Summer said, clapping her hands. "I have to admit, this is a lot more exciting when you actually know someone that's been nominated."

"You are looking beautiful tonight, Melanie. We're so glad that you were able to attend," said the bald man dressed in the three-piece suit. Was the man's collar too tight or did he always have that condescending look on his face?

"You know, John, that I'd never miss the chance to support my colleagues," his mother said as she turned and waved to another star before turning back.

"Well, we know that you have a lot going on right now. You've just finished filming and we understand that your son's girlfriend is in the hospital. I know that you have to be so proud of the two of them after that video of them helping to save that young boy came out," said the man.

"I can turn it off," Alex offered. Summer's excitement at seeing his mother in all her Hollywood glory had dimmed.

"I'm always very proud of Alex and Summer. They both are hardworking health-care workers. They make a difference in people's lives every day." Melanie smiled at the man and started to move on.

"Running away isn't going to help. Your mother can handle that weasel," Summer said, and then giggled. "He kind of does look like a weasel in that suit. Maybe you should give him the name of your publicist."

But this man, who from now on would be known as the weasel, had apparently forgotten about the other celebrities that were arriving. Instead, he'd chosen to follow his mother down the red carpet, his microphone still stuck in front of her. "There have been rumors lately of your son somehow being involved with the royal family of Soura. It seems that you were friends with members of the royal family before you moved to the States. Do you have any comments concerning these rumors?"

"Of course, there are rumors. There are always rumors. Isn't that how you make a living?" With no signs of hurrying, his mother waved a bejeweled hand at someone and with the flirty smile she had made famous, continued down the carpet.

Both he and Summe inhaled deep breaths as the camera followed Alex's mother until she disappeared inside the theater.

"It could have been worse," Summer said.

"I think you spoke too soon," Alex said as a photo of Summer and Alex taken from the viral video was suddenly displayed on the screen followed by a picture of Summer on the beach that had to have been taken only days before she had been admitted to the hospital.

"Where did that come from?" Summer asked. "Why would someone want a picture of me just walking on the beach?"

Something in Alex broke. The beach had always been her happy place. Her place of escape.

He'd tried to be nice. He'd given the interview he'd been asked to give. He'd ignored the reporter that had tried to ruin Summer's reputation instead of hunting him down. But still he hadn't been able to protect Summer from some stalker on the beach.

"Why me, Alex? I'm a nobody. According to one reporter I'm basically a gold digger. What is so interesting about me?"

He didn't need to tell her it was all because of him. She knew that. They both did. He turned the television channel until he found one of Summer's favorite shows.

"It will get better." But he wasn't sure anymore. No matter how many times his publicist assured him that it would.

"We can't keep trying to hide from them. All of this," Summer said as she raised her hands toward the television. "It's not our life. I won't have these babies raised in all of this."

Did that mean she wouldn't let their babies be raised around him? Could he even blame her for being worried after finding out someone had secretly been taking pictures of her? Because she was partly right. This wasn't her life, but it was his. It had always been his life; he had just chosen to ignore it.

"What do they want, Alex?" Summer asked,

her eyes focused so intently on him, as if he had the answer to make all of this go away.

And maybe he did. Maybe it was time to give the world what they wanted.

Summer thought she was ready. The doctors had managed to hold off her labor for three weeks. Each week the babies had stayed inside her had decreased their chances of complications, but it also increased the chance of infection from the ruptured membranes. While she'd been treated with antibiotics, the neonatologist and the perinatologist both agreed it was time for delivery.

Summer's only regret was that they'd have to go to the NICU as soon as they were born so they could be watched for any respiratory issues and to ensure they were able to maintain their body temperature. It made her sad and it wasn't the way she had imagined their birth to be, but she understood why the doctors were being cautious. Right now, all she wanted was her babies to be healthy.

Alex stood beside her as they draped her and began the procedure. Even with two NICU teams in the operating room, the room was extremely quiet. Alex held her hand and she squeezed his when she felt a tug at her abdomen.

"Are you hurting?" the anesthesiologist asked.

She shook her head as she watched Alex's face. A smile spread across it only a second before a cry filled the room. The doctor held the tiny, screaming baby girl over the drape for her to see before handing it to the waiting NICU nurse.

"And here's the second one," the doctor said as she once more felt a tug inside her.

When she didn't hear the answering cry, she looked up at Alex. He was concentrating so hard on something that Summer wanted to reach up and tear down the drape. Once more, a smile lit Alex's face, though she still couldn't hear the cry she wanted to hear.

"Here he is," the doctor said, holding up her son for her to see. Dark eyes blinked down at her. Eyes that she knew would someday match his father's.

"He's a serious one, isn't he?" the doctor asked before he handed him over to the waiting nurse.

"They're beautiful," Summer said to Alex as he strained over the operating table to see the nurses and their babies. "Go on. I'm okay. Go watch over our babies."

Pulling his eyes away from the babies, he

gave her a quick kiss and a fast "I love you," then headed across the room.

Summer knew it had been only a spontaneous sentiment. A flash of emotion with all the excitement of the day. How could he not feel emotional after such an experience as watching your babies be born? He didn't really mean it as he loved her like he was in love with her, no matter how much she wished it to be so.

Alex stood beside the wheelchair he'd used to transfer Summer to the NICU. While their daughter continued to expand her lungs with a cry that refused to be ignore, their son was being was sleeping quietly under the warming unit, where the nurses were continuing to monitor him.

"She's going to be a princess," Summer said.

"I know she is," Alex agreed.

"I didn't mean an actual princess. I meant she was going to be spoiled. You know, an everyday princess," Summer said. "Isn't it time for you to go?"

"Let them wait. It serves them right," Alex said.

"It's going to be okay," Summer assured him.

He straightened his tie and smoothed his

hands down his suit. "But what if it makes things worse?"

"Does it feel like a mistake?" his father asked as a heavy hand came to rest on Alex's shoulder. "I knew the moment that your mother and I agreed to keep your birth a secret that it was a mistake. At the time, with the way the country was struggling, it seemed the only thing to do. But I can tell you I have always dreamed of this day."

Alex straightened his shoulders. "Well, let's go do this then."

"Where's your mother?" his father asked. "She needs to be there by your side. We will show these fools that there is no weakness to be found here."

"We're not declaring war, Your Majesty," Summer said. Alex could see that she was holding back a laugh.

"As you say," his father agreed. "Let's get this over with. I want to spend some time with my grandchildren before I have to fly home."

"They're not letting—" Summer began before Alex cut her off.

"I'm sure we can arrange something," Alex said. Summer had a lot to learn if she thought that something as insignificant as hospital protocol was going to stop his father from seeing his grandchildren.

* * *

Alex wasn't surprised to find his mother entertaining the reporters that had been invited to the press conference. They'd been allowed to use the hospital auditorium only because it was separated from the main hospital, where patient privacy dictated a hospital policy of not allowing press on the premises.

As soon as he and his father entered the room, the hated cameras flashed until all Alex could see were yellow spots that clouded out the faces that shouted out questions in a rapid fire from all directions.

He could have had his father take the lead, but this needed to come from him. He would answer as many questions as possible and hope that once they had their answers, the reporters would leave with a sense that there was no longer a story here.

"Good afternoon. I want to thank you for coming today. I have some things to say and then I will take questions." He looked over at his father and his mother sitting next to him. No matter how this went today, he knew he had their support. He'd dreamed of being able to acknowledge who he was for as long as he could remember. Not the Prince of Soura, or son of the king and a movie star. He wanted to acknowledge that he was Christos and Melanie's son. How the media handled that was their problem. He only hoped that once this was out there would be no more reason for Summer and their children to hide from who they were: his family.

"Today is a special day for our family as we have just welcomed my daughter and son into this world." He waited as a smattering of clapping broke out in the audience.

"With these precious additions to my and Summer's life comes the responsibility of giving them the best life possible. Because of this…" He paused and looked to both sides. It was important for everyone to realize that they were a strong unit. There would be no stories going out that there was any discord between the three of them.

"We have decided that it would be the best of times to acknowledge that not only do I have the pleasure of being the son of the most talented star in the movie industry…" He paused again and waited for the blinding cameras to flash and another round of clapping to end until a silence settled over the room. It was like everyone in the room had inhaled a breath but was now afraid to exhale because they were too scared they might miss something. He'd never understand what drove these people.

"But I am also proud to be the son of His Royal Highness, King Christos Konstantinos of the House of Rothinburg." Alex took in a deep breath and let it out. It was done. There would be no more secrets about who he was. No more reason for these people to haunt his family. Or so he hoped.

He'd watched his mom deal with the media for years and one thing he had noticed was the way she worked to get them on her side of a story. He was counting on this working for him as well. He and his parents ignored the shouted questions that had immediately erupted from the crowd and waited for them to finally settle down so that he could continue.

"If you will all remember this all started because Summer and I were fortunately at the right place at the right time, and using our training, we saved the life of a young boy whom we both hope will go on to have a long and miraculous life. Even though the results of this act have interrupted our lives, we would never do anything different than what we did that day. It is what we do. It is who we are. We work each day in the hope to make our community, where we will now raise our children, a safe place for all. At no point have I or Summer ever desired to have our lives put into the spotlight that we now find ourselves in. It seems we have somehow gone from local heroes to a target for hurtful stories with no basis of truth and we can't help but wonder how this has happened."

His eyes searched through the faces of the reporters. Did any of them even understand the lines they crossed when they ran stories that could destroy other people's lives? Did they care? He had to believe that they did. There were reporters that were ethical in their reporting.

"Therefore, going forward, we request that you respect our privacy." Alex stopped and took a much-needed breath. This had to be the longest speech he had ever given. It would be the most important in his life. Now was the time to use one of the tricks his mother used.

"Look, guys, I understand the need for a good story. My parents will be answering your questions in a few moments and I'm sure what they have to say will be a lot more interesting than anything I'll say today. I'm a simple small-island doctor who has the privilege to be born to two wonderful people. Summer is a nurse who worked hard to get an education so that she could help others. Her job is to save lives and she's good at it. Let us do our jobs."

He started to leave, ready to end this, when he heard one question rise over the rest. "You refer to you and Summer as a family. Does that mean there will be a royal wedding in your future?"

Alex turned toward the man and smiled. Now this was a question that he didn't mind answering. "My greatest desire is to marry the love of my life and the mother of my children. Unfortunately, it seems not every woman is eager to marry a prince, so I have some work to do."

With that, he turned his back on the cameras and reporters, leaving his parents to handle them. He'd said what he had come to say. His parents would answer the rest of their questions, as well as inform the media that if there were any other attempts to interrupt Alex and Summer's lives, there would be legal consequences. They had decided that the threat would be taken more seriously if it came from two people who had the power to back it up. They weren't playing any more games. The media attacks had to stop.

Summer sat and stared at the television with Jo sitting beside her. Summer had informed, not asked, Alex that she would be telling her friend about his announcement before the press conference. She felt bad enough that she hadn't been able to share everything with her before now. She wasn't about to let her be blindsided by the news.

"Just, wow," Jo said. "This is too much. And that was so romantic."

Summer just stared at the television, unable to follow the questions as Alex's last statement had taken her breath away. Had he meant what he'd said? Did he really want to marry her, for her, or was this still just about wanting his children to have a father? Since the moment her water had broken, she'd shared every decision that had to be made about the babies with him. They didn't have to be married for him to be present in his children's lives.

But he'd called her the love of his life. The *love* of his life. And he'd declared it to the world, sharing something personal with a group of reporters that he didn't even trust. She'd never had someone love her that way.

"I'm going to go get another look at those beautiful babies," Jo said as the door opened, and Alex walked into the room.

"Are they still going at it?" Alex asked when he saw that his mother and father were still live on the local news channel.

How could he be so calm, when he'd just announced to the world that he loved her? That he wanted to marry her.

"You're wrong," she said, her thoughts pouring from her mouth before she could think better of it. "It's not that you're a prince. Where you came from has nothing to do with who you are now. I'm much prouder to have Dr. Alex as the father of my children then I ever would be to have any old prince."

"As where you came from has nothing to do with who you are," Alex said. He took a seat at the end of the hospital bed and took her hands into his.

"I know you don't care about that, but others…"

"I think I pretty much just told the whole world that I don't care what they think about anything. I love you and I want you to marry me. If not now, then a year from now. Or six years from now. I don't care how long I have to wait."

"But how do I know that it's me that you love? How do I know that you won't someday walk away from me?" Her heart wanted to believe him, but her head kept throwing up objections. Which did she trust?

Taking her hands in his, he placed them over his heart. "My heart beats for you and our children. That is not a love I can separate. But the way my heart races when I see you, the way your smile sends a jolt of joy through my soul, the way my whole body feels empty when I'm not near you, that is a love I have only for you, and it will never fade. I will always be there to take care of you no matter if you ever agree to be my wife."

The man slayed her with his words, words that mirrored her own feelings for him. Feelings that she had never been able to put into words. She knew so little about love that she didn't know how to describe it.

Suddenly a hidden part of herself, a part deep inside her heart that she had protected since the day she'd realized her father would never return, opened, letting loose a flood of joy and relief that she had never felt. If Alex had the same feelings for her that she felt for him, surely that meant that she could trust that he would never leave her. And she knew if she had a choice, she would never leave him. Oh, he might have to leave her for a week or a day, or even a month, but she would never doubt that he would return to her again.

"Yes," Summer said.

"Yes? As in 'yes, I'll marry you,' yes?" Alex asked.

"Yes, I'll marry you. Because I do love you, all of you. I love the doctor in you that risked your life to save another's. I love the man that holds me in his arms at night while we share our dreams for our children. I even love the prince in you who works so hard to make my dreams come true. I'll live beside you and work with you to give our children all the love possible. Because not only are you the doctor, the lover and the prince, but you will always be more than that."

"And what will that be?" Alex said before he pressed her hands against his lips.

"You will always be mine."

EPILOGUE

THE SOUND OF her heels echoed against the marble floors in the empty hallway. Holding up the front hem of her dress made from yards of white silk and lace, she could only walk so fast without tripping. It would never do for her to show up for her wedding in a dress with a tear, not after all the work Melanie and King Christos had gone through.

She glanced up at the white domed ceiling that was etched with gold vines. Was that real gold? It wouldn't surprise her if it was. She was so far from the little rusted trailer with the water-stained ceiling where she had lived as a child. At this point, pinching herself would do no good. It would take a full-on slap across her face to wake her from this dream.

Because it wasn't a dream. This was her new reality, for better or worse, or so the vows she was about to say said.

Finally reaching the door she sought, she

entered to find a room full of nannies along with a head nurse that the king had insisted on, even though Summer and Alex had assured him that his grandchildren were perfectly healthy and in no need of a nurse. They'd made it to three months old without any complications from their premature births.

"Is there something we can do for you?" the head nurse asked.

From the looks she was receiving, it was plain to see that they all thought her crazy. She was supposed to be downstairs in the grand ballroom marrying their new prince.

"I just need to see them," she said as she picked up the bottom of her dress again as she stepped over to the two matching cribs the palace had provided.

Each dressed in the white and gold colors of Soura, they looked like little angels as they slept. Or the little prince and little princess, as they now were.

"I thought this was where I might find you," King Christos said, entering the room. She tried to curtsy as the other women in the room did. As usual, she only felt foolish and awkward. Royal etiquette did not come easy to her even with the training she had received from her future mother-in-law.

"I'm sorry. I didn't mean to put you out,"

Summer said as the king took her hand, rested it on his arm and led her out of the room. Was the man afraid she was about to bolt?

"It's not that I don't want to marry Alex," she said. "I just can't help wondering how I got here."

"Well, that's simple enough. You fell in love with my son," the king said as they approached the double doors that led to the ballroom where Alex was waiting for her. He patted her hand and for the first time she felt that maybe the man understood her. She was just a simple woman with simple needs. "Are you ready, now?"

"Yes," she said as the doors opened and the crowd who had gathered to observe the marriage of Prince Alexandro and his bride rose from their seats. "I'm ready now."

The doors to the balcony opened. Alex, holding his son, Jacob Alexander Leonelli, and Summer holding their daughter, Margaret Marie Leonelli, stepped out into the sunshine and were greeted with cheers as his father presented the four of them as official members of the royal house.

A year ago, he would not have thought this was possible. Not the acceptance of his father's people, now his own people, or more importantly, the wife and two babies that made up his own family. Because all this pomp and ceremony was a wonderful change from hiding in the shadows of his brother and father. He no longer had to pretend that Nicholas was just a friend. They could be the brothers they were when no one was looking.

Most importantly, there were no more secrets between him and the rest of the world. His friends had taken the news with nothing but happiness for him. There had been no hard feelings because he had held back part of himself from people who had worked side by side with him.

"There is only one thing I want in this world," he said to Summer, who stood beside him waving to the crowd.

"And what is that, my prince?" she asked, her smile turned toward him now.

"To live out the rest of my life with you and our children," he said before bending down to kiss her lips.

"Of course, Your Highness," Summer said, "because everyone knows that a prince and princess deserve nothing less than to live happily ever after."

* * * * *